A Novel

THE GRAY BROTHERS

JOHANNA DELACRUZ

DISCLAIMER

All material is of mature content and theme. I advise reader discretion.

I would also like to acknowledge my husband, Chris Delacruz, for creating the cover of The Gray Brothers and supporting me with my writing.

I would like to thank my mother for suggesting this idea years ago regarding my family.

Thank you for your support to my family and friends who have supported and encouraged me to write.

The Gray Brothers are loosely based on family members from my dad. This book is to honor him.

CHAPTER 1

THE GRAY BROTHERS

Maggie

"Nolan! Give me back my bra, you little brat!" I chased Nolan down the hallway.

He ran while waving my bra in the air. You're wondering what I'm doing? I'm chasing Nolan Gray, the youngest of the Gray Brothers. He wasn't little since he's five inches taller than me, but he's still a pest.

Okay, you're confused about why I'm chasing him when I'm not even related to him. Why don't we backtrack?

Brian and Tricia Holloway, AKA, my birth parents, left a few weeks ago. They took a sabbatical for a whole stupid year without me, their loving daughter, and dumped me on our neighbors, the Grays. You're wondering why they didn't let me stay home. It's simple. They rented out our house.

I swear. Sometimes, my parents think of themselves.

Now, I have known the Grays since we were neighbors. Pat and Nate are the sweetest people you'll ever meet. Can they adopt me?

They're sweet. Nate and Pat's sons aren't. They are the biggest troublemakers on the block and are always causing problems. The biggest problem is that they're freaking hot. Even Nolan is cute. It's the one thing they have going for them. How do they have the parents they have? It's beyond me.

Nate and Pat exude kindness. And the Gray Brothers are the demon spawns raised from hell's depths. In case you're wondering, no, we don't get along. The hatred between us is mutual. It's been that way the entire time I have known them.

The brothers hate me; I hate them; We hate each other. The worst part was that I went to school with each of them. I experienced my gawky teenage years, only for the Gray brothers to pick on me. Hey, they weren't always hot. They had their moments.

Nash Gray was the oldest. Next was Nixon. Then the demon twins, Nathan and Noah. Never confuse the demon twins. I did once, and they never let me forget it. I do it to spite them— finally, their baby brother, Nolan, who's the devil incarnate.

I endured living in their house for the past two weeks since my loving parents dumped me on them. It's been a change.

"Stop taking Maggie's underwear, Nolan." Pat snatched my bra from him and tossed it to me while passing him in the hallway.

"Aw, Ma. You're no fun."

"When you have kids, then you can be no fun." She shrugged as she walked away and winked at me. I couldn't help but giggle. I love Pat.

I walked into my bedroom.

"Dear diary. I saw Bryson today, and he's so dreamy, as always. Oh, did I tell you? I'm the most boring person on the face of the earth?" Nathan asked, peeking up from my journal.

"Give me that," I said, reaching for my journal.

Nathan yanked it away. "No offense, but I got bored after five minutes of reading this crap." He tossed the book aside.

"Oh, let's leave boring Betty alone, Nathan. She enjoys being boring." Noah flipped through a magazine.

"Get out!" I pointed at the doorway.

"Gladly," Nathan said, getting off the bed. They left the room. The twins are hell's demon spawn and as bad as Nolan.

A door slammed with heavy footsteps thumping up the stairs. I peeked out of the doorway and got met with, "What?"

"Nothing."

"Do you need to stare at people?"

"Who pissed in your Cheerios?"

"Forget it. Stop staring. It's creepy."

I shot Nixon a glare, and he gave one back. Great, Nixon was home. Let the fun begin. Yeah, senior year will be an exciting year.

It's the story of how the Gray brothers changed my life while I changed theirs.

CHAPTER 2

NASH GRAY

Maggie

I was in a deep slumber until someone bumped into furniture while cussing up a storm. Ugh, I'm glad someone thinks of other people needing sleep. I propped myself up. I noticed a silhouette bumping into items and throwing stuff around the bedroom.

Oh, you don't worry, buddy. I enjoy watching a guy invade my room while making noise. He stopped and made his way over to the bed, falling onto it. What the hell?

I pushed him with my finger. "Hey, buddy. You're in the wrong room." He didn't budge. So, I tried to shake him until I heard snoring. Oh, hell, no. I was not sleeping next to a dying bear. Not to mention, I didn't even know this guy.

My theory is that he needs a good night's sleep if he's planning on killing me. If he didn't kill me, then we have a huge problem. I tried to make my great escape until a hand stopped me. The person yanked me onto the bed, engulfing me with their muscular arm.

I don't mind a muscular arm around me, but I prefer it to be with someone like Bryson Tilson. Thinking about him sent my heart racing. I haven't gotten the nerve to talk to him yet. This year will be the year.

"Will you shut up? I'm trying to sleep. Your yapping is keeping me awake," the person said through the muffled sound of the pillow with their face buried.

"Well, excuse me, but you barged into my room while I was sleeping."

"You mean my room."

"Um, no. It's my room."

He lifted his head. The moonlight hit his face, showing his hair flop upon his forehead. "Nope, this room has been mine for the last twenty years. Now shut up and go to bed. We can discuss sleeping arrangements in the morning." He threw his head back into the pillow.

Well, shit.

Lying next to me was none other than Nash Gray, the oldest of the Gray Brothers. He's twenty and has been away for the past year. Pat said he needed to find himself. He needed to find a personality. He's hot, but he's like a sack of wet potatoes, useless like his personality.

I refuse to sleep here with him. I got up, yanked down, and pulled to him. Then he inhaled. "Mm, coconuts."

Did he freaking sniff me? Why the hell is this guy cuddling me? We hate each other.

I drifted off to sleep after I stopped trying to leave. It didn't matter because Nash kept pulling me back into the bed.

I awoke the following day to notice Nash changing his clothes. His personality might be an ass, but he sure had a nice one.

"Take a picture. It'll last longer."

"What?"

"I said take a picture since you enjoy staring at my ass so much."

I gave him a disgusted look as he smirked.

He pulled a tee shirt over his head. "I'm glad you outgrew your ugly duckling stage, Maggie."

"Was that a compliment?"

"Sure, let's go with that." He rolled his eyes at me.

"Shouldn't you be finding yourself or something? I doubt you found your personality. You need to leave and go find it again."

"Ouch." He placed his hand over his heart, feigning hurt. "Should that offend me? It didn't. Then again, your presence here is offensive enough."

My blood boiled.

"Don't get mad. I mean, it's not like we haven't caught you staring at us through your bedroom window."

"I wasn't staring."

"Whatever helps you sleep at night. You need to find another bed to sleep in tonight." He walked out of the room.

Fantastic. I deal with the jerks who lived here and now with the king jerk himself. Ugh. My parents could not come home soon enough.

CHAPTER 3

NIXON GRAY

Maggie

I climbed out of bed and changed my clothes before going downstairs. As soon as I walked out of the bedroom, I ran smack into Nixon. He gave me an annoyed glance.

"You can't be serious. You can stare at us, but you can't look where the hell you're going. Get out of my way." He brushed past me, bumping his shoulder against mine.

Nixon Gray was the second oldest brother, who's eighteen, and hated the sight of me. We're seniors this year. Lucky for me, I get to see him and his charming personality at school and at home. Woo hoo!

Nixon was the most unpredictable of the brothers. He gets into fights, expresses an opinion, and hates me. What did I do to him?

The only time he acts sweet to someone is towards his mom or a girl he was dating. The only two times that I've seen his pleasant behavior.

Then there were his brothers and Dad. He would be in an in-depth discussion with Nash or talking to his dad. Nash and Nixon have always been close. They plotted about how to make my life miserable.

Nixon wouldn't be a terrible guy if he had a better temperament. He's hot but doesn't have much else going for him.

I came downstairs for breakfast. The brothers had eaten it by the time I appeared.

"Oh, Ma and Dad left early, so they made breakfast. Sorry, you took your sweet ass time getting down here," Nixon said, smirking while his brothers snickered. I shot him a glare as he took a bite of bacon and grinned. I wasn't too fond of Nixon.

He was moody, rude, condescending, and any other dreadful thing that comes to mind. I had to find something to eat before we left for school. I scoured the cupboards and fridge for food, not seeing many choices. I decided on toast. At least, it was something.

As I waited for my toast, the four of them, besides Nash, got up and left. Good. I didn't want to deal with them. The toast popped up. The engine roared in the driveway as I was getting ready to butter it.

"I would hurry. Nix gets impatient with tardiness," Nash said.

"He wouldn't."

Then he peeled out of the driveway.

"Oh, he would." Nash smirked.

I walked to the door. Yep, Nixon left. Great. Now I had to walk to school. I grabbed my toast, slapped butter on it, and made my way to school. As I munched on my toast, I planned ways of getting even with Nixon all the way there. If he wants to play dirty, then I'll play dirty. I'm friends with a specific female he has been checking out at school.

I made it to school as the Gray brothers laughed at me. God, I hate them. I strolled to my locker as Kat and Marcy walked up.

"How is life at the Gray house?" Marcy asked.

I glanced at her. "It's jail."

"Yeah, with hot inmates," Kat said.

I rolled my eyes. The brothers walked by. I caught Nixon checking out Kat. Hmm. It's the perfect time for revenge.

"You won't believe what I found out," I said.

"What?" Kat asked.

I leaned into them and whispered. Both Kat and Marcy's eyes got huge, and both said, "Nah, uh."

"Yep." I nodded my head.

"Damn, that's a shame because they're fine-looking specimens," Kat said.

"Oh, and spread it around," I said.

"Don't worry. We will," both said.

They walked to their class as I walked to mine. Check and mate, boys.

CHAPTER 4

NATHAN AND NOAH GRAY, DOUBLE THE HOTNESS

Maggie

I noticed the Gray twins heading right towards me as I walked to my classes. They didn't seem happy.

Nathan and Noah Gray looked identical but were fraternal twins. Unless you meet them, you can't tell them apart. You call them by the wrong name, lookout. Noah was taller than Nathan.

They had turned seventeen and were juniors in high school. They're a pair of pain in the asses and like to give me a hassle. They also had a temper.

"Well, hello, boys," I said.

"Don't hello, us," Noah said.

"You're the one who started that stupid rumor," Nathan said.

"I don't know what you mean." I feigned ignorance while pleading the fifth.

"Cut the crap, Maggie. You told your two big-mouth friends that we're gay," Noah said.

"Gay? I didn't realize that you're gay. Well, that explains so much."

"This isn't funny, Maggie!" Nathan said.

"Oh, well, I'd rethink your lifestyle choices." I pushed past them with a smile plastered on my face. The twits shouldn't have eaten all the breakfast and let me walk to school.

The twins were as evil as the others. Their specialties were pranks. When I first arrived, they had tossed my underwear all over the yard. So, I got even and put itching powder in their boxers. It gave a whole new meaning to the word jock itch. We fought during the past two weeks.

Their faces were priceless. Revenge was so sweet.

At lunchtime, I was having lunch with Kat and Marcy when someone slammed their palms on the table. We saw the Gray boys standing there with Nixon front and center, glaring at me.

"What can I do for you, boys?" I asked.

"I'll give you two seconds to take it back and tell everyone the truth," Nixon said.

"Or what?" I stood up and placed my palms on the table while challenging him.

"Or we'll tell everyone your little secret," Noah said.

"What secret?"

"The one where you have the hots for Bryson Tilson," Nathan said. "That is that dork's name, right?" He asked Noah.

"Yep," Noah said.

"You wouldn't."

"We would," Noah said.

Nathan nodded his head.

I had to think for a moment. Do I tell the truth? The Gray brothers will still have leverage to hold over my head. Do I try another tactic? I pondered my options, tapping my finger against my lips. I'm going with Plan B.

"Okay." I stepped on the seat at the table. "Attention, everyone! I must be truthful about the Gray brothers! They're not gay! I repeat, they're not gay!" I noticed the brothers had a smug expression. "But they have an STD! A nasty one! They call it the Clap!"

I glanced at them as their jaws dropped open.

I leaned toward them. "Tell Bryson. It's not like any girl will touch you with a ten-foot pole."

"Oh, it's war," they said.

"Bring it on, boys," I said.

Yep, a war got declared between the Gray brothers and me. That should be entertaining.

CHAPTER 5

NOLAN GRAY

Maggie

With war declared between the brothers and me, who knew what would happen now? Nolan moved in for the kill. I walked to my locker when someone said, "Hey, Tits McGee! Did you lose something?"

I turned around to see Nolan twirling one of my bras around on his finger. Where did he get my bra, and how did he bring it into school?

"Nolan! Give me back my bra!" I chased after him.

He bolted while holding my bra.

Let me explain about Nolan. He's fifteen and a sophomore in high school. He's the family's baby and has a perverted side to him. One time, I caught him watching me change. I wanted to dropkick him in the nuts.

I ran after him, but he ran faster. When I reached him while trying to catch my breath, the brothers raised my bra on the flagpole. They let my C cup flap alongside the flag. I wanted to kill them.

"Well, that's a fascinating new flag," a voice said.

Oh, God. Please let it not be him. I turned, and sure enough, Bryson Tilson stood next to me with his backpack flung over one shoulder. My crush saw my black, lacy bra flapping in the wind. Now I want to die.

I turned and walked away while the boys smirked. That was it. Tonight, I was no longer staying with the Grays. I didn't care if I slept in the garage at my house. I refuse to spend one more night with those disgusting boys, even if they're freaking hot.

By the time I got to their house, they had beaten me there. I walked into the kitchen.

"My brothers told me that you saluted the entire school," Nash said with a smirk while the rest snickered.

Without saying a word, I walked past them.

"Oh, please don't go away mad. Just go away!" Nixon said, causing them to laugh.

I hurried up to Nash's room and packed my stuff. After ensuring I had all my belongings, I carried my bags downstairs.

Nolan caught me leaving. "Where are you going?"

I didn't look at him. "Why do you care? You guys win. I'm leaving." I walked out and closed the door.

He walked to the door and opened it. "Come on, Tits McGee! We were only messing with you! Come back, Lassie. Come back!"

I didn't bother answering. The brothers made it clear that I'm not welcomed here.

While I was busy running away from home, the brothers would meet issues with my disappearance act. I would learn this later.

*****

Nash

"Who are you yelling at?" I asked.

"Maggie." Nolan shrugged.

"Why did she leave?" Asked Nixon.

"Because she left."

Nixon and I glanced at each other. "What do you mean she left?" I asked.

"Well, she was carrying bags and left. What do you think I mean when I say she left?" He rolled his eyes at me.

My brothers and I ran up to my room, finding Maggie's stuff gone. I started pacing, running my hand through my hair. "Damn it."

"So, she left?" Noah asked.

"No, she's here but invisible. Yeah, she left!" I spoke.

"Ma and Dad will kill us," Nixon said.

"No shit, Sherlock! We need to find her before they get home," I said.

"Boys, we're home!" Ma said.

We glanced at each other with wide eyes. "Nolan!" We raced downstairs to find our parents with Nolan.

"Boys, where's Maggie?" Ma asked.

"Funny story," Nolan said until I silenced him with his hand.

"Um, we have to go pick her up from her friend's house," I said.

We dragged Nolan out of the house, saying bye to our parents.

If we didn't find Maggie and bring her back before our parents learned she had left, the shit would hit the fan. Good luck to us. We'll need it.

CHAPTER 6

THIS SUCKS

Maggie

I needed to stay somewhere else, and I thought about my garage. The renters might have an issue with a stranger staying in the garage. I made my way to a bench, took a seat, and set my bags down. I dug through my purse, trying to find money, then found cash. I collected whatever cash I had.

After collecting every single piece of cash, I counted it. I had eleven dollars, which would get me food. A hotel room was out of the question. I sighed, rubbing my forehead. My stomach started growling, and I decided on nutrition. I stood up and grabbed my bags.

I walked, finding a mom and pop's restaurant. I walked in, sat in a booth, and set my bags by me. I pulled a menu from a holder and flipped through it. I decided what I wanted when a voice asked me, "What can I get for you?"

I noticed Bryson holding a notepad and pen. My eyes widened. "C-coffee."

He arched an eyebrow and wrote down my order. "Is there anything else?"

"Um, um." I didn't know what to say. Bryson stood there, waiting. "Um, can I have a turkey sandwich, too?"

He scribbled on his pad and walked away. That couldn't have gone any worse. Coffee and a turkey sandwich? Who the hell orders that combo? No wonder he was giving me a weird look.

I sat there. A few minutes later, Bryson returned with my food and drink, placing them in front of me.

"Anything else?"

"Can I have a Coke instead of a coffee?" I gave him a sheepish expression.

He smiled at me. "Sure. It surprised me that you ordered a coffee."

"Lack of judgment." I shrugged.

He chuckled as I smiled. He took my coffee and exchanged it for a Coke. I sat there, eating my sandwich, as I watched Bryson. He flitted from booth to booth, waiting on tables. At one point, he glanced at me and winked. My cheeks warmed.

After eating and drinking my Coke, I sat there. I was trying to hold off leaving until I had no choice. The diner was closing. I grabbed my stuff and left. Bryson was locking up when he noticed me. He walked over to me. "Are you going somewhere?"

I glanced at my bags. "Oh, these? I'm going to my friend's place."

"Aren't you staying with the Grays?"

"Well, I was, but Nash came home. So, they don't have the room. My friend offered for me to stay with them." I plastered a fake smile upon my face. He gave me a strange glance but shrugged.

"Well, catch you later, Coke and a turkey sandwich."

I stood there as he walked away. Did he call me by my order? I knew everything about this guy, and he called me by my order. Perfect. Bryson won't remember me, and I doubt he even cares. Well, this sucks.

Okay, well, my crush doesn't know I exist. The brothers chased me out of the place I was staying. I'm getting short on cash. I can't stay with Marcy or Kat since they don't have the room either. Thanks, parental units, for dumping me and having your vacation.

As I contemplated my pathetic existence, I would learn a valuable detail about the Gray brothers.

*****

Nash

I drove, searching for Maggie as the sky turned dark.

"Where the hell would she go? It's not like she has many options," Nixon said.

"How the hell should I know? It's not like I know that much about her," I said.

"Who cares? Isn't this what we wanted?" Nathan asked.

I skidded to a stop and threw the car into the park. Nixon and I turned to him. "Listen, you panty wise. We were having fun. I never meant for her to leave," I said.

"Is it my fault that she can't take a joke? No, it's not." Nathan glared at me.

"That's not the point," Nixon said.

"Then explain the point because I'm sure we'll piss off Ma and Dad when they find out," Noah said.

"The point is, she's a major pain in the ass. She's creepy and always staring with those big blue eyes that sparkle when the light hits them a specific way," Nixon said. He noticed us giving him strange expressions. "What? Don't tell me you haven't noticed her eyes? Yeah, I thought so." He turned around and shrunk into his seat.

I looked straight ahead and started driving. "Or her hair that smells like coconuts."

"Or her stupid perfect white teeth," Noah said.

"Or her annoying beautiful laugh," Nathan said.

"Or her perfect......." Nolan said.

I slammed on the brakes as Nathan and Noah smacked Nolan.

"Nolan, you're such a perv," Nixon said.

Nolan shrugged. I drove around until I found Maggie sitting on a bench with her bags. She had her chin in her hand while sitting there.

I pulled up and parked the car. "Stay here." I walked towards her with my hands shoved into my jean pockets.

Maggie sighed as I stood in front of her. "Don't worry. I'm not coming back. I'm trying to figure out a place to stay."

I gazed at her.

"You can leave. I'm sure you wouldn't want to leave your precious bed cold."

"Are you always this bitchy, or is that your charming personality?" My deep voice surprised her.

She crossed her arms. "Are you always a dickless asshole?"

"Get in the car."

She peered around me to find my brothers waving at her with smirks. Then back at me. "I would rather get smacked in the face with a dead fish than get into a car with your brothers." She pointed past me.

"Stop being a pain in the ass. Get in the damn car!"

"No."

"Yes."

"No."

"Yes."

"No."

"Yes."

"No."

"No."

"Yes. Wait. What?"

I waved my brothers out of the car. They walked up, grabbed her bags, and carried them to the vehicle.

"Wait! I didn't agree to this!" She gestured at them while stomping her foot.

"Sure, you did."

She didn't respond until I tossed her over my shoulder and carried her to the car. I handed her to Nixon, who shoved Maggie into the car. She kicked Nixon.

"Ow! Quit it!" Nixon said.

"Get your hands off of me!" Maggie spoke.

"Nash, can we put a gag on her and tie her wrists and ankles?" Nixon asked.

We looked at each other. Maggie gulped. Yep, we gagged her, then tied her wrists and ankles.

"Much better," Nixon said with relief.

Maggie shot Nixon a glare as I laughed.

CHAPTER 7

SNEAKING IN

Maggie

"How will we get past Ma and Dad with her bound and gagged along with her stuff?" Noah asked his brothers.

"Are you thinking what I'm thinking?" Nash asked Nixon

"Oh, yeah," Nixon said.

What is these twits planning?

"What?" Nolan asked.

They smiled. "Little brother, you're getting a lesson in the birds and the bees," Nash said.

"Why would I want that?"

"Cause if you don't, we'll tell Ma about your stash of Playboys," Nixon said.

"Pft, big deal. Ma already knows."

"Does she know why her Victoria's Secret catalogs keep disappearing?"

"You wouldn't."

"Oh, but I would." Nixon smirked.

"Fine, but you guys are real dicks." Nolan got out of the car. There's nothing like blackmail between brothers to show that you care. I must hand it to the Gray Brothers. They'll play dirty with others. It's nothing compared to what they do to each other.

Nolan knew more about sex than any fifteen-year-old. It's a miracle for him to agree. I didn't want to know what he did with his mom's Victoria's Secret catalogs or my bras.

"Nolan's talking to Ma and Dad in the living room. Nix will help me with Maggie. Noah and Nathan get her bags. We'll take her upstairs through the back way," Nash said.

They got out of the car. On our way inside, they stopped and checked to see how poor Nolan was fairing.

Pat and Nate were thinking about what they wanted to say. Nolan sat there, trying to act innocent. This kid was far from innocent.

"He'll kill us for making him sit through that conversation," Nixon said.

"Yeah, well, he deserves it. It'll teach him to keep himself in check," Nash said.

They carried me and my bags upstairs and took me to Nash's room. Noah and Nathan tossed my suitcases onto the floor, and Nash and Nixon tossed me onto the bed. Geez, they could have been gentler.

"Now, we'll untie you and remove your gag. You won't yell or scream. If you kick me, I'll tie you to the bedposts. Got it?" Nash asked me.

I nodded. I didn't want the brothers to tie me to Nash's bedposts or any bedposts.

They undid my ties and gag as I stared at them.

Nixon leaned into Nash. "I told you that it's creepy when she stares."

Nash shook his head and rolled his eyes. "Okay, it's time to set some ground rules."

"Ground rules? Ground rules!" I stood up. "What ground rules?" I started pacing while tapping my finger against my lips. Then I pointed to each of them, beginning with the twins. "You invade my privacy by reading my journal and going through my stuff." Next was Nixon. "You're rude to me every chance you get. You're more volatile than a girl on her monthly. And you." I stopped at Nash. "You kicked me out of your bedroom. You haven't been home for over a year. Oh, and let's not forget Nolan, the little pervert he is. But I need ground rules."

I sat in a huff. The brothers didn't want me here, and I didn't want to be here. Lucky for me, my loving parents dumped me here.

Nash took a seat next to me. "Okay, we have been a little rough on you."

My face snapped in his direction. "A little?"

"Okay, a lot. In our defense, it's not like we had a girl in the house except for Ma. So, it's new to us."

"I'm an only child whose parents aren't around. I'm staying in a house with seven people. It's not a walk in the park for me either."

"Well, we have to figure something out. I'm sure Nolan will blow our covers in about five seconds," Nathan said.

"I give it three," Noah said.

"What?" Someone asked.

We stopped and looked at the door.

"What do you mean you know about sex?"

"Yep, we're dead," Nathan said.

We heard thumping against the steps, along with running. Nolan ducked his head into the room. "Sorry, boys. But you're on your own." He left. A door slammed, with more footsteps following.

"Oh, boys. We'd like a word with you." Pat's voice was sweet, which made it creepy.

"I'll kill him," Nixon said.

"Boys, a word now." Nate waggled a finger at them.

He and Pat stood in the doorway.

The brothers sighed as they left the room. I couldn't help but wonder what Nathan meant. What did they do? As they say, curiosity killed the cat, but satisfaction brought it back. I made my way to the top of the steps.

I heard yelling and cussing. I didn't realize Nate knew so many cuss words. He always seems so laid back. Pat was even worse because she looked like such a sweet person. While it was amusing to watch them sit on the couch and cringe, I was getting tired.

I strolled back to Nash's room and grabbed my stuff. I needed a place to sleep. I headed to a room that they didn't use. I flicked on the switch to view a room they used as storage. In the corner was an old cot. I'll use that.

After moving stuff around, I set up the old cot and rummaged through my stuff, finding a pair of sweats and a hoodie. I changed into them and turned off the light. Then I crawled onto the cot and fell asleep.

Nash

Once our parents finished screaming at us, we headed back to my room. "Okay, Maggie," I said.

We found her and her stuff gone.

"Where'd she run off to?" Nixon asked.

"Gee, I don't know, Nix. Siberia. How the hell should I know?" I asked.

"She's in the storage room."

We turned to notice Nolan eating a candy bar.

"Why?" Nixon asked.

"Beats me." He shrugged and walked away.

We made our way to the storage room, flicked on a hall light, and saw Maggie asleep on the old cot. She wore a pair of sweats and a hoodie without a pillow or blanket.

"We're sort of dicks," Noah said.

"No, little brother, we are dicks," I said. "Come on."

My brothers followed me to a closet. I pulled out blankets and a pillow, handing them the items. "It's time to stop being dicks and give the girl a break."

We returned with the items. We placed the pillow under Maggie's head and the blankets over her while trying not to wake her. Once we finished, we left. I stopped and turned to Maggie. "Night, Mags."

As I left the room, I heard. "Night, Nash." I stopped and smiled. A little kindness goes a long way.

*****

Maggie

The following day, I awoke, got dressed, and headed downstairs. I looked for bread to make toast.

"There's breakfast for ya," Nixon said.

A plate of food sat on the counter. Okay, what was the brothers' game?

I turned to them. "You didn't poison it, did you?"

"Yeah, sure, and have Ma and Dad kill us. Yeah, I don't think so," he said.

I picked up the plate, walked over, and took a seat by Noah. I dug in, and it was still warm. It's so much better than toast.

Nathan said, "Come on. We don't want to be late."

Okay, what's with the brothers? Did they fall and hit their heads?

We walked to the car, and they offered me the front seat.

"Will you get in? If we're late, Ma and Dad will kill us," Noah said.

I took a chance and got in. Nixon started the car and roared out of the driveway. I wasn't sure about these boys. I'm sure they're plotting something. I needed to figure out their game. With the Gray Brothers, their acts of kindness come with strings.

I didn't realize what strings they were, but the brothers would forever change my life.

CHAPTER 8

GENUINE KINDNESS OR A GAME

Maggie

So, the entire week, the brothers have been decent to me. Even Nolan had stopped stealing my bras. Living with them wasn't too bad. They still had their moments, but I got used to them.

Seeing the brothers in action was even better. It fascinated me to see the boys bicker over everything or threaten to hurt each other. It's better than me.

I needed a break from the boys, so I hung out with Kat and Marcy. Sometimes, you need more estrogen when you're stuck in a house full of testosterone. One girl can take so much farting and burping.

I left for the day. The boys had other plans, which I would discover when I returned.

*****

Nash

"Will she like it?" Noah asked.

"Well, gee, Noah. We won't know until we do some work," Nixon said.

"Dude, you need to chill. You're worse than a chick on her period," Nathan said.

Nathan earned a glance and punched from Nixon.

"Leave Nix alone. He gets sensitive at the time of the month." I walked by, carrying stuff.

"Nash, he's always sensitive. The dude cries at chick flicks," Noah said.

"I do not!"

We stopped and stared at Nixon.

"It was one time! Geez. You cry at a poignant scene, and everyone loses their freaking minds." He threw his hands up in exasperation.

We rolled our eyes and shook our heads. Yep, Nix's a drama queen.

We carried stuff to the attic, clearing out the extra room. After clearing out most of the boxes and items, we found a bed.

"Ma likes to put stuff everywhere," Noah said.

We stood there, looking at the bed.

"Well, let's grab clean sheets and blankets. Nathan, strip the bed, and the rest of you finish up. She'll be here in an hour," I said.

"Why should I strip the bed?"

"Because I said so, or I'll give you an atomic wedgie. It's your choice." I gave Nathan a knowing expression.

"Bed it is," Nathan said.

I had no issue doling out punishment to my brothers. Nathan brought in sheets, a blanket, and pillows for the bed. We made the bed, getting the hell out of there.

*****

Maggie

I returned to the house, wanting a nap. I like Kat and Marcy, but it's Saturday, and I enjoy my sleep. I walked up the stairs, and the doors closed. I headed to the storage room, opening the door. My eyes widened to see the clutter gone. The room was clean with an actual bed.

Doors opened as the brothers stuck their heads out before sneaking over to the room to watch me.

The room isn't significant. At least, it's something.

Nolan leaned into Nash. "Does she like it?"

Before Nash answered, I said, "I don't like it."

Their faces dropped.

"I love it."

A smile curled upon their lips. They stepped from behind the doorway and entered the room.

"We figured you could decorate it your way," Nash said.

I turned to face them.

"Yeah, we're not good with that girl stuff," Nathan said.

"I can manage," I said. "There's one slight problem."

"What's that?" Asked Nash.

"I need to go shopping and need someone to take me."

The brothers shoved Nash towards me. He turned and shot them a glare as they looked around and whistled. He exhaled a deep breath and turned to me. "Fine. Don't make shopping an all-night project." I grabbed his hand and led him out of the room.

"Nash will kill us," Nixon said.

"Yep, because he hates shopping," Noah said.

"Sucks to be him." Nathan shrugged.

Ten minutes later, Nash pulled into a parking lot, and we got out of the car, heading into the store. Since my parents abandoned me, I'll use their credit cards. They're for emergencies only. A lovely room is an emergency. Well, it is for me.

We grabbed a shopping cart. Nash pushed it and leaned on the handle while I looked at things. We didn't talk while I shopped. I mean, it's Nash. He's a high school graduate and three years older than me. We had never spoken except when I was younger. That was basic stuff.

"So, what things do you like?"

"Oh, this and that." I checked out stuff, trying to ignore Nash's attempt at a conversation.

"Anything specific?"

"Nope." I picked out a couple of pictures that I liked. "What do you think?" I held up the pictures.

"They're doable. Not what I expected."

"And what did you expect?"

"I don't know. Like pink items, bunnies, or some shit like that."

"Contrary to trendy belief, girls are born with a uterus, but that doesn't mean we gravitate to pink stuff and cutesy animals." I placed the pictures in the shopping cart. "Why do people make assumptions when you're a specific sex? People label you if you don't live up to those theories."

"Because it's our culture. Well, at least, in the States. People in Europe don't care about half of the things we do. Sure, they have problems. They're way more cultured than we are." He pushed the cart as we moved down the bedding aisle.

"I'd like to go to Europe one day."

"Let me guess. Paris, France?"

"Nope. I want to visit Austria or Germany. It's the food and beauty of it all." I let out a sigh. "But that won't happen if it's up to my parents."

"Why do you say that?"

I gave him a glimpse. "They took a sabbatical and left me with the neighbors. They didn't want me to miss school or tag along on their trip."

"That is a little harsh. Don't you think?"

"The same people prefer money over me. My babysitters were more like parents to me than my parents. When I had birthday parties, my parents would hire sitters to be them."

"So, the people we saw in your yard weren't your parents?"

"Nope. They were my babysitters."

"That makes more sense than what we assumed."

"What did you assume?"

"Your dad had many wives."

I laughed. "Your theory was a much better story and sordid." I smiled as Nash laughed.

We finished shopping and returned to the house. I put a few pictures on the wall, improving it.

Pat stopped by to see the bedroom. "The boys did an outstanding job."

"Yeah, it surprised me when I came back to see the room cleaned."

She walked in and looked around. "Well, be happy. The boys never did that for anyone."

"What do you mean?"

"I don't know if you've noticed. My boys aren't the nicest, and outsiders don't last. Consider it a gift."

"Should I worry?"

"God, I hope not." She giggled.

Her remark didn't make me feel better. It's like the other shoe would drop, and I wondered if it's a game with them. Be friendly to the outsider. Gain their trust. Make them seem like an idiot.

Pat left the room as I stood there. I didn't want to let my guard down with them. Heaven knows what they had planned for me next. I didn't want to stay in the room. What if they pull a prank, steal my clothes, or invade my privacy? Ugh, I needed to find another place to sleep.

I'll sleep on the couch. If I'm in the open, the brothers can't do anything to me. Their parents would catch them. Yep, that's what I'll do.

I packed my stuff and continued down to the couch in the living room. I carried the blanket and pillow I bought. Nope, I'm not falling for the brothers' kind act. The Gray brothers were never pleasant for a reason. There were always strings attached.

Not today, boys. Not today.

CHAPTER 9

TO FAKE OR NOT TO FAKE, THAT IS THE QUESTION

Maggie

I slept on the couch, snuggled in the blanket I had bought.

"Explain to me. Why did we do all that work so Maggie would sleep on the couch?" Nixon asked.

"How the hell should I know? It's not like I can read minds," Nash said.

"Should we wake her?" Noah asked.

"Yep," the brothers said.

Nathan pulled out an air horn and put it by my head. He pressed the button, causing me to scream and fall onto the floor. I shot them a glare. They smirked at me.

"What is wrong with you guys?"

"What's wrong with us? We should ask you. We put much work into that room, and you're sleeping on the couch," Nixon said. "So, enlighten us. Why are you here and not there?" He pointed upstairs.

I can't let them know that I was onto them.

I stood up. "I saw a spider."

"A spider?" Nathan asked.

"Yes, it was big and hairy. Did I mention big?"

"Fine. Someone will kill the little bugger. Then you can sleep in your room," Nash said. "Kill the spider, Noah."

"Why do I have to do it?"

"Because I said so."

"Fine, but the next one, Nixon gets." Noah stomped out of the room.

Well, shit. That didn't go as planned. I prayed the Gods would take mercy on me. Then a scream erupted with Noah flying down the stairs.

"Yeah, no. That was one big ass spider." He looked like he saw a ghost.

And the Gods have answered my prayers.

"It can't be that bad," Nathan said.

"Then, you kill it!" Noah said.

"Fine, I will, you pansy." Nathan headed upstairs.

We waited until he came flying down the stairs.

"Screw that! That thing is mammoth!" Nathan said.

"I can't believe you two are afraid of a little spider." Nixon took care of what they couldn't upstairs. A minute later, he came barreling down the stairs, tripping. "Yeah, not going to happen."

"Are you serious?" Nash asked.

"Yeah, I am. I don't know how it got there. But it needs to go back." He pointed with a head turn.

Nolan was the next one, and he was as bad. "Nope, nope, nope."

Nash headed upstairs to investigate. "Someone, get me a bat!"

How giant was this spider? I checked for myself, trudging upstairs. They followed me. I glanced at the hairy thing, then flew out of the room.

"That thing is gigantic!" I hid behind Nixon, who pushed me in front of him. I swear to God that these guys were absurd. I'll get eaten by a spider, and they'll stand there and watch.

The six of us stood in the hall. We argued about who would kill the stupid spider. Pat walked by us, took a shoe, and whacked the spider twice. We stopped.

She walked by us. "All this commotion over a little spider." She shook her head and laughed.

We stood there. What happened? We got shown up by Pat. That's what happened. When I asked the Gods to send me a spider, Big Bob from Arachnophobia was not what I meant. Now I didn't want to sleep in the room. Period.

Pat had Nate check the room for any more spiders. They didn't find any. Thank God, because I doubt I'll sleep in a spider riddle room. It would never happen.

After taking my stuff back to my room, the boys felt it would be nice to spend Sunday afternoon with me. I had other ideas of enjoyment, like fantasizing about Bryson.

"And what do we have here?" Nathan jerked my journal out of my hand and plopped on my bed. "Oh, Bryson. You're dreamier than most guys." I tried to get my journal back, but he moved it out of my reach. Then he held me back with one hand as he continued to read. "Why won't you notice me? You would like me. Pbttt." He made a jerking motion with his hand.

I yanked my journal out of his hand. "Do you mind?"

"Drop it, Maggie. That tool won't even notice you," Noah said.

"You don't know that. He talked and winked at me the other day," I said.

"Did he have something in his eye?" Nathan asked.

I gave Nathan an annoyed look.

"He could have had something in his eye."

I shook my head. "Bryson will notice me. I need to get the courage to talk to him."

"Okay, then do it tomorrow," Noah said.

"I will," I said.

"Good."

"Fine."

"Now we settled that. Can we not discuss that tool?" Nathan asked.

"What tool?" Nixon asked, walking into my room.

"Bryson Tilson," Noah said.

"He's not a tool," I said.

"Oh, he's a tool. He's the definition of a tool. Open a dictionary and go to the word tool. You'll find Bryson's picture," Nixon said.

"He's not a tool," I said.

"Trust us. Bryson's a tool," Nathan said.

"What are you guys talking about?" Nolan asked while entering my room and eating a sandwich.

"Bryson Tilson," Nixon said.

"That tool?"

"Even Nolan realizes he's a tool," Noah said.

"Nolan assumes that everyone's a tool," I said.

"This is true," Nolan said. "But Bryson is the biggest tool. Trust me. The dude spends more time looking in a mirror than he studies."

"I'm not having this argument with you guys."

"Fine. We'll make you a deal. You get Bryson to ask you to Homecoming, and we'll leave you alone," Nixon said.

"On one condition," I said.

"What's that?"

"If he takes me to homecoming, you four have to wear a dress for an entire day at school." I narrowed my eyes and smiled.

"Fine," Nathan said.

The brothers jumped on him by agreeing to my terms. I'll go to Homecoming with my dream guy, and the Gray brothers will wear a dress to school. I can't wait. Now to figure out how to get Bryson to go with me.

I had to figure out how to approach Bryson. I tried out novel approaches in front of the mirror. I was trying to find the one who worked the best.

Then someone said, "If you want to get a guy's attention, be yourself." Nash leaned against the doorframe with his arms crossed.

"What's wrong with the approaches I've done?"

He walked into the room towards me. "They're wrong and fake. Guys like girls who are themselves."

"Well, being myself got me nowhere. Bryson looks at me like I'm invisible."

"Okay, pretend I'm the guy you like. Hit me with your best shot."

I loosened up my shoulders and moved my head around as I closed my eyes, trying to gain confidence. Think of Bryson. Think of Bryson. I chanted to myself.

"What are you doing? Preparing for a fight? Relax."

"Fine." I opened my eyes. "Hey, Bryson. Remember me from the diner? My name is Maggie."

"Maggie, who?"

"Maggie Holloway."

"Who?"

"Maggie. We go to school together."

"Never heard of her." He shrugged.

"Forget it." I turned to walk away when Nash caught my arm.

"Okay, okay. Sorry." Nash chuckled. "Try again."

I sighed. "Hey, Bryson. Remember me? I saw you working at the diner."

"Oh, yeah. How have you been?"

"I'm good. Do you want to go to Homecoming with me?"

"Yeah, sure." He shrugged.

"Oh?"

"Yeah."

"Great!" I smiled. "That'll work. Thanks, Nash." I wrapped my arms around his neck, taking him by surprise. His body tensed, but he relaxed and wrapped his arms around my waist.

"Sure, Mags."

I let go as he lingered, looking into my eyes. I stared into his steel-grey eyes.

"Yeah. So, thanks for your help."

"Sure, no problem. I'll see you later." Nash left my room.

I bit the tip of my thumb. Did Nash and I have a moment? Nah, that's Nash, and Nash doesn't have moments. At least, I don't assume he does.

Forget Nash. Focus on Bryson and the boys wearing a dress for an entire day. That would be fun.

CHAPTER 10

GETTING NOTICED

Maggie

The next day at school, I gathered my courage and talked to Bryson. What's the worst that would happen?

He was standing at his locker, and I took a deep breath. I'll walk up to him and say hi. It wasn't a big deal.

I walked toward him. My heart was pounding, and my palms were sweaty. I reached him. "Hi, Bryson."

He glanced at me. "Do I know you?"

"My name is Maggie, or the girl who ordered a Coke and turkey sandwich."

"Oh, yeah! You ordered a coffee, then switched it to a Coke. I remember now. How have you been?"

"I'm good." I smiled. Well, so far, so good. "So, I was thinking Homecoming was coming and."

A girl interrupted me, walking up to Bryson. "Hey, babe." She kissed him.

"Hey, baby," he said. "What were you saying about homecoming?"

"Um, Homecoming is coming, and you're going with this girl." I pointed at the girl.

"Well, she is my girlfriend. Are you ready?"

"Yep."

They walked away.

"Who was that girl?"

"Beats me," he said.

My heart sank. Can you say crash and burn? I had pined for this guy for four years. He didn't know who I was except for my order. Great. I had to figure out about Homecoming. I couldn't tell the brothers that Bryson had a girlfriend, and I didn't get the chance to ask him. I would never hear the end of it.

It's time to plan, which would take finesse. I didn't need the brothers to find out.

Later that evening, I was working on my homework in my room.

"So, how did it go?" Nash was leaning against the doorframe.

"It went great! He said, yes!" I faked a smile.

"That is great. I hope you have a wonderful time with Bryson."

"Yeah, I have to finish my homework."

Nash got the hint and left. Now to keep up the ruse, which would take work.

*****

Over the next few weeks, I played it off about Bryson. I always made an excuse about having to meet him. At school, I acted as if the guys had missed him. I couldn't reveal the truth. They would never let me live it down. I won't confess that I had crashed and burned.

While I figured things out, the brothers had other ideas, which I would discover later.

Nixon

"I say we have a brief chat with the tool," I said.

"Yeah, but it'll piss Maggie off if she finds out," Noah said.

"Who cares? We're watching out for her, right?" Nathan asked.

"Right," we said.

"Um, guys."

"Not now, Nolan," I said.

"But guys." Nolan pointed at someone.

We saw Bryson with a girl.

"What the hell?" Noah asked.

"Oh, hell, no." I marched towards Bryson with my brothers following me. "Yo, ass-munch! What do you think you're doing?"

Bryson turned to us. "Excuse me?"

"You heard me. Why are you messing around on Maggie?"

"Who's Maggie?"

"The girl you're talking to and taking to homecoming," Nathan said.

"What do you mean? The only girl I'm talking to is my girlfriend." He gestured to the girl with him.

"What?" We asked.

"Yeah, my girlfriend, whom I'm taking to Homecoming. I don't know any Maggie." He looked at us like we had lost our minds.

"Our bad. Forget what we said," Noah said.

"Gladly." He rolled his eyes as we walked away.

"Why would she lie to us?" Nathan asked.

"None of this makes sense," I said.

"She could feel embarrassed. Bryson was her crush," Noah said.

"Whatever. Bryson's a tool," I said.

"So, does this mean we don't have to wear a dress?" Nolan asked.

"That's what it means, little brother," I said. "Now I have plans for our precious Maggie." I smirked while rubbing my hands together.

"This ought to be good," Nathan said.

"This is what we'll do."

I whispered my plan to my brothers.

*****

Maggie

I was at my locker when someone said, "Attention, everyone! Maggie Holloway has been fooling us!"

I saw the boys standing in the middle of the hallway. What did those idiots have planned?

"Maggie has a crush on Bryson Tilson!" Nathan said.

Oh, no. My eyes widened as Bryson walked up with his girlfriend.

"So, everyone should learn how much she likes him!"

Nathan pulled out my journal. Oh, God. "Oh, Bryson is dreamier than most guys! He's so special compared to other guys! I hope that he asks me to Homecoming!"

Everyone stared at me, including Bryson, who looked embarrassed. I glared at the brothers. At that moment, I hated them. I shut my locker and walked away, feeling humiliated.

"Don't go away mad!" Nixon said.

I'm so done. The Gray brothers humiliated me, having read my thoughts to everyone, including Bryson. I walked to their house. As soon as I reached the front door, I ran past Nash and up to my room, slamming the door shut. I wasn't staying here any longer. They were nothing but a bunch of jerks. They were demon spawns, and I refused to stay here any longer.

As I packed, the boys came into the house while laughing.

*****

Nash

I met my brothers as they came into the house. "What happened?"

"Oh, it's payback for Maggie lying to us and getting us to wear a dress." Nathan snickered.

"What did you guys do?"

Nathan pulled out my journal and tossed it to me. "It was brilliant. Nixon came up with the idea."

I caught the journal. "You took Maggie's journal?"

"Nash. You should have seen her face. It was priceless," Nolan said.

Then my brothers stopped talking and laughing as Maggie came down the stairs. Their smiles faded.

"Mags. Where are you going?" I asked.

Maggie stopped. "Ask your loving brothers. They read my journal in front of everyone at school, including Bryson. I'm glad that you found it funny. Was it great? Did you enjoy humiliating me in front of everyone? Yeah, I lied, but I would have never done what you did. I hate you!" With that, Maggie left.

I tapped the journal against my palm. "So, you thought humiliating Maggie was the best choice?"

"Come on, Nash," Nixon said.

"Grow up. It's one thing to mess with someone, but what you did was asinine." I tossed the journal at them, walked past them, and out of the door.

*****

Maggie

"Maggie!" Nash caught up to me.

I turned around. "What?"

"My brothers are idiots. Please don't leave."

"I can't go back to school, Nash. Not after what they did." Tears fell down my cheeks.

"I can help you. Come back inside, and I'll fill you in about my plan." He held out his hand. I handed him my bag. He threw an arm around my shoulder as we walked back to the house.

After returning to the house, Nash and I were up in my room.

"So, why did you lie?" Nash took a seat on my bed next to me.

I shrugged. "I was afraid of what you guys would do."

"Well, no offense. If a guy can't remember a girl like you, he's a tool."

"That's what your brothers call him."

He chuckled. "Sounds about right."

"It was humiliating. I was going to ask Bryson to Homecoming. I had to figure out how to get myself out of it." I blew air past my lips.

"Well, I wouldn't worry about Bryson Tilson. He doesn't realize what he's missing."

"I guess." I shrugged.

"One day, you'll meet a guy and realize why it never worked out with anyone else. Give it time."

"I suppose."

"Let me tell you what I have planned for the four yahoos."

Nash told me his plan. It was genius, and they deserved it. I couldn't wait.

CHAPTER 11

PAYBACKS ARE A BITCH, AND SO ARE YOU!

Nash

"I can't believe we're doing this! This is such bullshit," Nathan said.

"Yeah, well, I don't like it either. So, suck it up, buttercup," Nixon said.

"This is ludicrous," Noah said while shaking his head.

"Um, you guys want to get moving. You're prolonging the inevitable and making it worse," I said. "Now, go on. Show the world who you are."

"Come on, Nash. We said that we're sorry," Nolan said.

"Well, baby brother. Sorry, don't cut it. A little humility will help you and your egos." I patted his back.

My brothers waited until the hallway was full of students when the boy's bathroom door opened. They ran out buck naked through the halls, yelling they were sorry to Maggie.

Maggie stood there, laughing.

I exited the bathroom and joined her. "So, do you approve?"

"I was all for the dress idea. But your idea is so much better. Thank you." Maggie stood on her tiptoes and kissed my cheek.

I smiled. We watched as my brothers streaked the school.

Today my brothers had learned a lesson in humility and how far they went. Because of their streaking, everyone forgot about

Maggie's journal and her crush on Bryson, except for Bryson. He walked down the hallway to see Maggie talking to me. The view piqued his interest.

*****

Nixon

My brothers and I finished Nash's punishment. We ran back to the boy's bathroom to get dressed. As we dressed, we talked.

"I still can't believe Nash made us do that." I button my jeans.

"Well, can you blame him? We didn't think this whole payback through," Noah said.

"Yeah, you're right. Maggie only lied because she assumed we would make a big deal out of it," I said.

"We did. We read Maggie's journal in front of the entire school," Noah said.

"I still can't believe she likes that tool. What guy doesn't remember someone like Maggie?" Nathan asked.

"A tool," I said.

We laughed while leaving the boys' bathroom. We weren't aware someone was in the bathroom as the last stall door opened with Bryson stepping out.

*****

Maggie

Nash's plan of making the boys' streak through school was brilliant. Then again, they are the Gray brothers. If they don't plot, I would wonder about them.

I filled in Kat and Marcy with what happened, and they laughed. We were talking when someone tapped my shoulder.

"Nixon, it's all your fault." I turned, not to see Nixon but Bryson.

"Hey, Maggie," Bryson said.

My heart raced. "H-hey, Bryson." Bryson always made me nervous. The past four years had been that way.

"Do you have a date for homecoming?" The words escaped his lips, taking me by surprise.

I stared at him. This can't be real. "I thought you were going with your girlfriend?"

"We got into a fight, so I decided to ask you. What do you say?" He gave me a toothy grin. God, his teeth were perfect. Focus, Maggie.

"Uh."

My friends elbowed me.

"Yes."

"Great." He walked away, then stopped and turned. "But we'll have to meet there. I have to take care of things first."

"Yeah." I smiled.

He shot me a smile and walked away. I turned to my friends. "Oh, my God." I squealed, as did they. We jumped up and down. Bryson asking me to Homecoming made me ecstatic. My crush of four years asked me to Homecoming. I can't wait.

Bryson

While I left that loser in a dreamlike state, I met Tiffany.

"Did she buy it?"

"That was way too easy. Now we wait for Maggie to show up. The Gray brothers want to humiliate me. I'll humiliate her. Plus, the way she stares at me is creepy."

"No kidding."

Maggie

Yes, ladies and gentlemen, my dream guy wasn't dreamy. When you experience a major crush on a person, you overlook the awful things about them. You focus on the good. It would be a lesson I would learn the hard way.

The girls and I shopped for dresses for Homecoming. We found apparel, shoes, and accessories for Homecoming. I wanted to look special for Bryson and found a navy blue, chiffon, knee-length dress with a pair of navy heels. I couldn't wait to wear it.

We headed back to the Gray house, hanging out in my bedroom. I worked at breaking in my shoes. I didn't need blisters at the dance. As I walked around my room, Nixon walked by, spotting us.

He stopped and popped his head inside. "Ladies."

"Hey, Nixon," the girls said.

He strolled inside. "Nice shoes."

I turned my foot. "Yeah, I'm hoping to break them in before Saturday, or my feet will hurt."

"That would suck." He tried to act cool in front of Kat because he liked her.

I wasn't too fond of Nixon for understandable reasons but took pity on him. "So, Kat, did you find a date for homecoming?"

She gave me a 'what are you talking about expression.' I gave her a 'go with it' nod.

"Ah, um, nope. No date yet. I figured I would go alone." Kat picked up what I was throwing down.

"That is a shame. Nixon doesn't have a date either." I draped my arm around his shoulder. Yeah, if looks could kill, I would be dead.

"Oh?" She feigned surprise. "Nixon doesn't have a date. I don't have a date. We could have no dates together. Then we wouldn't dance alone, at least. But, whatever."

I nudged Nixon, who cleared his throat. "Yeah, we can go together because of the dancing."

"Good."

"Fine."

"Great." She tapped her fingers on her knee.

"Uh, well, I have to go. What's that, Ma? Did you say that you needed my help? Be right there!" He left as we laughed.

"Thanks, Maggie."

"What?"

"There's nothing like putting the poor boy on the spot." She smirked.

"Oh, come on. You have liked Nixon forever, and he likes you. If I can get a chance with Bryson, you can get a chance with Nixon."

"You're right." She smiled.

"Well, you both have dates, and I'm the low man on the totem pole," Marcy said.

"Isn't Keith taking you?" Kat asked.

"You mean that no good, dirty dog, cheating, slimy asshole."

"Wow. Tell us how you feel," I said.

"Never mention that name again," she said.

Keith was out. Cheating on one's girlfriend helps.

Then an idea hit me. I walked over to the doorway. "Oh, boys! Can you come here for a second?"

"Maggie, what are you doing?" Marcy asked through gritted teeth.

"You'll see."

Noah and Nathan walked in a few minutes later. "What?" Nathan asked.

"My friend over here," I pointed to Marcy, "needs a date to homecoming."

"Yeah, so?"

"Which one of you would like to take her?"

"I'm out." Nathan didn't give it a second thought.

"I'll take her," Noah said.

"What?" Nathan asked Noah.

"Dude, she's hot! Why wouldn't I take her?"

"Because I don't have a date."

"Who cares? You said no, and I said yes. It's your loss."

The demon spawn argued as I shook my head.

"Hey!" I cut off their bitch fest. "Marcy has a twin whom Nathan likes."

"No, I don't!"

"Shut up. Yes, you do. Marcy, call your sister and put her on speakerphone."

Marcy shrugged, pulling out her phone and dialing her sister. Macey picked up after the second ring.

Hello?

"Mace, it's me."

I know who it is, dumbass. I have a caller ID. What do you want?

"Would you like to attend homecoming with Nathan Gray?"

That fool? You can't be serious!

"Yes, that fool, and I am serious. What do you say?"

The other end became quiet as we awaited her response.

He is hot so that I can overlook his foolishness for a night. Yeah, sure. Why not? It's not like I have better plans.

"Great." Marcy hung up.

Nathan was turning three shades of red. Did I mention Marcy and Macey were twins? Oops, I forgot that little tidbit.

Each of us had a date for Homecoming, including Nolan. He was a horn dog and let no grass grow under his feet.

I can't wait because this Homecoming will be one we wouldn't forget. It would be worse for me than anyone. I didn't realize it yet.

CHAPTER 12

HOMECOMING HUMILIATION

Maggie

We got ready for Homecoming. Kat helped me with my hair and makeup. I let my excitement get the best of me, bouncing around in my seat.

"Will you stop moving? Your eye makeup will look like a cat."

I laughed.

"Maggie!"

"Okay, okay." I tried to stay still. Kat finished, and I looked in the mirror. She did a fantastic job. "Kat, you need to go to school for makeup."

"Yeah, I'm thinking about it." She put her makeup tools away.

I got up from my chair as Marcy and Macey were finishing. The boys were waiting downstairs for us. The girls had gone ahead while I checked my lipstick one last time.

"Wow, you look amazing." Nash was leaning against the doorframe.

I smiled at him. "God, I hope so. It took Kat over an hour to do my makeup." I walked toward him.

"You have a wonderful time tonight."

"I plan on it. I get to go to Homecoming with my dream guy. What else is better than that?" I beamed.

"Well, I hope that he treats you right, or he'll answer to me." He leaned towards me with his breath fanning my face.

I detected a hint of vanilla and became dazed but snapped out of it. "Um, I better get going."

"Yeah, you don't want to keep the tool waiting. I mean, Bryson."

I rolled my eyes. None of the boys liked Bryson if you couldn't tell. I didn't even understand why.

We walked downstairs, and I joined everyone else as we made our way to Homecoming. A surprise awaited us, going down in the history books about why the boys didn't like Bryson. I would soon find out.

*****

We pulled up in the limo, getting out. We walked inside, making our way to the dance floor. I searched for Bryson, finding him by the punch bowl.

"There you are."

"Here, I am."

"So, would you like to dance?"

"Yeah. Why don't we have a drink?" He smiled.

Everyone made their way to the dance floor.

"Punch?" He gestured at the punch bowl.

"Sure." I smiled.

Bryson poured me a cup of punch and handed it to me. I took a sip as a liquid poured over my head. Punch covered the floor around my feet.

People stopped to watch the altercation.

Tiffany walked around, holding an empty cup in her hand, and kissed Bryson.

Then he turned to me. "Why would I go out with someone as creepy and hideous as you?"

I stared at him in horror.

Then he started screaming at me. "God, you're pathetic! Oh, Bryson, you're dreamier than most guys. Oh, Bryson, why won't you look at me? Bryson, you and I would be better together than most couples. Sound familiar?"

Oh, God. He was reading a copy of my journal.

"Oh, wait. It gets better than what I've read. Bryson, I would do anything for you. To have your body against mine, to savor your lips."

I snatched the paper from his hands as people stared at me in stunned silence. My breathing increased as my cheeks burned.

"Are you serious? Did you think I would drop my hot girlfriend for someone as ugly as you? That is so funny. Don't you think that's funny, Tiff?"

"It's hilarious."

"I'm going to go."

"Yeah, you do that."

I turned and made a hasty retreat, leaving the Homecoming dance.

*****

Nixon

We saw Maggie leaving the dance humiliated while covered in punch.

"Okay. We did nothing like what that tool did," Nathan said.

"That tool signed his death warrant," Noah said.

"Why would he do that?" Nolan asked.

"Because he's a complete, utter Dickless, asshole," I said.

"So, are we going to stand here?" Nathan asked.

"Nope. We'll have some fun." I cracked my knuckles.

While we took care of Bryson, the girls took care of Tiffany. Yeah, it turned into one hell of a homecoming.

*****

Maggie

I walked home, sticky and feeling like absolute shit. I brushed tears away from my eyes. At one point, I took my shoes off. I had wasted four years on a boy. The boys were right. Bryson was a tool, and I needed to burn that damn journal when I got home.

I got back to the house, and Nash was sitting in the living room. I needed to sneak past him and not let him catch me. He would laugh because that's what the Gray brothers did. They enjoyed my misery.

I had gone through the back. When the coast was clear, I made my way upstairs until Nash stopped me. "Mags? Why are you home so early?"

I froze in my spot, hearing his deep voice. I didn't turn to face him. "Oh, I wasn't feeling good."

"Are you sick?"

"Something like that. I'm going to take a shower."

"Okay. I hope you feel better."

I hurried up the stairs. Thank God it was dark. He didn't see me covered in punch. I made my way into the bathroom, turning on the shower. I undressed and stepped in. The water cascaded over me as I washed the punch off me, then cried.

One guy ruined my senior Homecoming memories and humiliated me. FML.

*****

Nixon

"Ma and Dad will kill us for getting suspended," Nolan said.

"Yeah, but it was worth it," I said.

We sat in the principal's office and waited for their parents to show up.

*****

Nash

"Where are you going?" I asked his parents.

They walked towards the front door. "Well, your brothers got into a fight at the dance," Dad said.

"All of them?"

"All of them, including their dates," Ma said.

"Why?"

"We're not sure. Your brothers said something about a tool deserving it. I didn't realize the school had tools at Homecoming," Dad said.

My dad could be dense.

"Dad, a tool is what you call a guy when they're an asshole."

"Nash Nathaniel Gray! Language!" Ma said.

"Sorry, but it's true."

"Well, tool or no tool. We have to pick up your brothers," Dad said.

They both left the house.

I sighed, knowing what had happened. It was easy to figure out why Maggie was home early, and my brothers were in deep shit. I walked upstairs and came to Maggie's shut door. I knocked.

"Come in."

I opened the door to find Maggie shoving her shoes and dress into a garbage bag. "Mags?"

"Oh, hey, Nash. I was cleaning up. What's up?"

"What happened at the dance?"

"I told you. I wasn't feeling good. But I'm better now."

"Then explain why my brothers are sitting in the principal's office, and my parents have to get them."

"That happened after I left."

"Are you sure?"

"I'm positive."

A few minutes later, the front door opened with yelling coming from downstairs.

"I don't care whether the guy is a tool or not! It does not give you the right to beat the hell out of him!" Dad said.

"But he deserved it!" Nixon said.

"And you deserved to get suspended for three days!"

"But Dad! You didn't see what he did to Maggie!" Nathan said.

"I can gather a good guess. It still doesn't mean that you take matters into your own hands!"

"But Dad!" Noah said.

"Enough! Go to your rooms! We'll discuss your punishment later!"

My brothers stomped up the stairs.

"You try to do one good thing for someone, and you get the shit end of the stick," Nathan said.

"Yeah, but now he knows what it's like to mess with someone we care about," Nixon said.

My brothers agreed.

"Now, will you tell me what happened?"

Maggie sighed. She told me what had happened. To say I was beyond pissed didn't even describe half of it. I couldn't help but take his brothers' side on this one and go to bat for them with our parents. My parents were in the kitchen, sitting at the kitchen island, drinking coffee. I explained to them what had happened.

"That poor girl," Ma said.

"I understand you want to punish them. Nix and the others were only doing what they thought was best for Mags. Go easy on them this time."

My dad sighed. "Fine. But they're still getting punished. How is Maggie?"

"She's heartbroken. Dad, she hides so much. Her parents don't care, and the guy she liked turned out to be a douche."

"Nash."

"What?"

"Be careful, Nash. She's a sweet girl."

"Trust me, Dad. I get it." I walked away.

*****

Pat

"What?" Nate asked me.

"Did you forget you're older than me?"

"No, I haven't forgotten. You remind me every day." He sipped his coffee.

"It wouldn't be a bad idea if Nash and Maggie ended up together." I shrugged.

"Pat, I know what you're planning, and stay out of it

"Oh, Hunny. You know that I can't do that." I patted his shoulder.

"Yeah, that's what I'm afraid of." He drank his coffee.

CHAPTER 13

HEARTBREAK

Maggie

People say heartbreak comes in many forms. My heartbreak came at the expense of humiliation. If someone doesn't like a person, let them down gently. Don't humiliate them to the point of no return. It's so not cool.

My friends tried calling me. I refused to answer their calls. The brothers tried to talk to me, but I refused to speak to them. I didn't need to feel any worse than I did.

Someone tapped on my door.

"Go away, Nash!"

"It's not Nash, sweetie. It's Pat. Can I come in?"

I sighed and answered the door. Pat stood in my doorway, waving her hand to her side. Her head turned to the side as I stared at her. Then she gave me an innocent smile.

"Let me guess. The brothers put you up to this."

"I don't know what you mean."

Liar.

"Fine. Come in. Only you, not the boys."

I heard a collective aww.

She walked into my bedroom. I closed the door, sat down on my bed, and grabbed a pillow while hugging it.

She took a seat next to me. "Maggie, please talk to me."

"What do you want to say, Pat? I liked a guy for four years, and he detests me. Or that he humiliated me last night. Take your pick."

"Maggie, the boy you liked wasn't the boy for you."

"Why does everyone keep saying that?"

"Because we see things that you don't. Think about it. We ignore the terrible traits when we like someone, focusing on the good. Sometimes, we focus on those things and ignore what is right in front of us."

"What do you mean?"

"Nate and I didn't always get along. We hated each other at one point."

"But you guys are the perfect couple."

"Well, we didn't start that way. We were neighbors, and he has two brothers. Nate is the oldest of seven years. I grew up with one older brother and his friends. So, I dealt with more testosterone than estrogen."

"I didn't know that."

"Yep, Nate and his brothers used to pick on me as big brothers would do to their little sisters. I hated them." She spoke in a throaty tone.

I laughed at her exasperation.

"But then, one day, it changed."

"What happened?"

"Well, I liked this boy. I thought he was my dream guy and tried to talk to him. It didn't go well. He degraded Nate and his brothers, with me taking exception. Our interaction got heated, and I ended up on the receiving end. Well, Nate found out. When Nate and his brothers got done, the guy regretted his decision."

"He didn't?"

She nodded. "Oh, he did. Nate gave him a free nose job several times. We talked, getting to know each other. After I turned eighteen, he asked me out. He wanted to wait so that it wasn't weird. It scared him."

"It didn't scare me!" A voice said through the door.

"Oh, hush!"

"Well, woman! If you tell a story, then tell it right!"

"I am! Now pipe down!"

They made me laugh.

Then Nixon said, "Hey. Ask them if they want ice cream."

"Isn't it the wrong season for ice cream?" Noah asked.

"It's never the wrong time for ice cream. You give girls chocolate when it's that time of the month and ice cream when they're upset," Nathan said.

"Who told you that?" Nash asked.

"Well, that's what Dad does for Ma," Nathan said.

"He has a point," Nixon said.

Nate sighed. "How about if we get some ice cream?"

"Do they think ice cream will cure a broken heart?" I asked Pat.

"It might not cure it, but it'll help."

"Can we get chocolate sprinkles and whipped cream?"

"We can get whatever you want, sweetheart!" Nate said.

"Fine." I grabbed my sneakers and put them on. Ice cream isn't the answer, but it's a start.

We got up from my bed. Nate and the brothers were smiling. I rolled my eyes, walking past them. There goes my wallowing in my self-imposed misery.

*****

After we got our ice cream, we sat at a couple of tables. When Pat pushed Nash to sit with me, I sat, enjoying my ice cream. He sighed and walked over, taking a seat across from me.

"What?" I took a spoonful of vanilla ice cream, shoving it into my mouth.

"Nothing." He shrugged.

"Why are you looking at me that way?" I arched an eyebrow.

"You have whipped cream right there." He pointed at my face.

"Where?" I checked my face.

"Right here." He took whipped cream from his sundae and touched my nose with it. He smiled as I glared at him.

"Well, you have whipped cream on yours." I grabbed whipped cream and rubbed my hand over his face. His family stopped and watched us.

"You need some chocolate sauce to go with that." He flung chocolate syrup at me.

"Well, you can't have a sundae without the ice cream." I picked up my treat, smashing it into Nash's face. Then we caked each other with our ice cream while I squealed. When we finished, we started laughing.

"Come on, giggles and chuckles. You both need showers."
Nate ushered us to one car. We laughed at each other, cracking
jokes in the vehicle.

*****

Nixon

"Is there a reason you did that?" I asked Ma.

"Nix, we need a push to realize who is right for us."

"Says who?"

"I say. Trust me. I know what's best." She smirked while
walking away and getting into another car.

"What happened?" Nathan asked me.

"Ma happened."

"Well, damn."

"Does this mean we have to help her?" Noah asked.

"What do you think? It's Ma."

"So, I can't steal Maggie's bras anymore?" Nolan asked.

"Not if you want Nash to kill you," Nixon said.

"Bummer." Nolan shrugged.

"Boys! Hurry! Damn. You four are slow as molasses!" Ma said
from the car window.

"Yes, Ma," we said.

*****

Maggie

Once we got to the house, Nash and I showered. I needed to get the stickiness off me — that damn Nash. He started it. If anyone has ever had whipped cream dry on them, it's like rubber cement, trying to get it out of your hair. I got it out of my hair and cleaned the sundae's sticky residue off me, then got out of the shower.

I dried off and put on dry, clean clothes, then brushed my hair. This shower is what I needed. I walked out of the bathroom, and Nash came out of his bedroom.

"All clean?"

"Yep, although I don't want to wash the whipped cream off me again."

"Well, I got ice cream where you shouldn't have it."

I laughed.

"I take it you're doing better."

"A little. Having your heart crushed by your crush isn't fun, but I'll survive."

"He's a tool. From what Nix said, he won't feel or look too hot in school tomorrow."

I snickered. As we walked downstairs, I asked, "Is it terrible that I'm glad your brothers rearranged Bryson's face?"

"Nope."

I laughed even more. It's funny. The Gray brothers and I never got along. Now, I have a newfound respect for them. It was the start of a beautiful friendship.

CHAPTER 14

FALL FESTIVAL CARNIVAL

Maggie

After Homecoming, the Grays were right. Bryson didn't look as hot as I thought he did. A broken nose and two black eyes will do that for you. His girlfriend looked rough. Did I feel bad for them? Nope, not one bit.

People forgot what happened to me at Homecoming. Bryson showed up at school, resembling Frankenstein's monster. Well, he has a good Halloween costume. He didn't need makeup.

I looked at posters plastered around the school about the fall festival carnival. I always go with my friends since there isn't much to do here. We took a moment to have fun. As I studied the poster, someone said, "Oh, great, another carnival." I turned and glimpsed Nixon standing next to me.

"You're not going?"

He snorted. "Oh, hell no! You won't catch me dead there."

Kat and Marcy walked up. "We won't catch you dead where?" Kat asked.

"Oh, Nixon considers carnivals beneath him," I said.

"Oh? I love them."

"A person can change their mind," he said with a slight smile.

I giggled at how he changed his tune with Kat.

"Are you going?"

"I wouldn't miss it for the world."

"Cool. I'll catch you there. We must head to class before we're late. Later, Mags. Later, Nixon."

"Later, Kat." I turned to Nixon. "So much for not going."

"Oh, shut up." Nixon walked past me.

I laughed. It was amusing to watch Nixon turn to Jell-o around Kat.

*****

Pat

"A carnival? Those things are lame," Nathan said.

"Well, too bad. You're going," I told the boys.

"But Ma!" The boys said.

"No. We don't do anything as a family. With Nash home, I want to spend time with my family."

Maggie came into the kitchen.

"It's your fault," Nathan said.

Maggie stopped. "What's my fault?"

"Because of you, we have to go to that stupid carnival," Noah said.

"Okay, first, I didn't even know you were going. Second, my friends and I go every year," Maggie said.

"Pft, whatever," Noah said.

Maggie and Noah argued.

Nash came into the kitchen. "Why are you two fighting?"

"Well, thanks to Maggie. We're going to the carnival," Nolan said.

"What's wrong with a carnival?" Nash asked.

"They're lame," Nathan said.

"You're lame, but we're not complaining about you, are we?"

Nathan shut up.

It didn't matter how much they whined and complained. The boys were still attending.

*****

Maggie

At the carnival, I hung out with my friends. Well, that was until Nixon stole Kat away from me. I shook my head and rolled my eyes. The twins grumbled until Marcy and Macey asked them if they wanted to ride the rides with them. They changed their tune. Then there was one.

Nash and Nolan hit the rides together, as did Pat and Nate. Great. Everyone had someone to ride the rides with except for me. I walked around, trying to figure out what to do. Most rides require a partner. I got stuck with a schmuck who didn't have a partner. That was my luck of late.

After two rides, I got a refreshment and found a picnic table on the carnival grounds. As I sat alone, Bryson and Tiffany walked up. Even better.

"It's Maggie without her bodyguards."

Will someone please explain why I had liked this tool for four years?

"The brothers are here."

"Where? Because I don't see them."

"Don't worry. The brothers are around."

"Thanks to them, they broke my fucking nose!"

"Oh, well, you shouldn't have read my journal, you douche."

That pissed him off. I wouldn't let Bryson bully me.

He stalked towards me as I got up. He took a swing at me. I hauled off and hit him with my fist, causing him to step back.

"You bitch! You re-broke my nose!" He grabbed his face in pain.

"It improves your face, but you have a shitty personality. So, I doubt it."

He got his composure and took another step toward me before someone caught him.

"The lady has spoken once with her fist. You may not want to feel her answer again." Nash held Bryson's arm.

Bryson jerked his arm away and stormed off, with Tiffany scampering behind him.

"Well, we know you can handle yourself."

"I can't believe that I liked that tool."

We laughed.

"Where's Nolan?"

"Little shit found a girl."

"Oh."

We stood in awkward silence.

"So, do you want to ride the Ferris wheel?"

"Sure." Anything was better than awkward silence.

We stood in line and entered the ride, getting into a bucket. The ride started. I hated the Ferris wheel but didn't tell Nash that little detail. I didn't need him to tease me.

"It hasn't been a bad night, has it?"

"I rode the rides with a schmuck. Then I dealt with an ex-crush. Yeah, sure." I sighed.

"Yeah, I guess it's sucky."

"It's the story of my life."

"Have you been to the funhouse?"

"What?"

"The funhouse. Have you gone through it yet?"

"No, and that's one carnival attraction I visit."

"Good. After the Ferris wheel, we'll go through the funhouse."

The Ferris wheel rotated twice. We exited, heading to the funhouse. It was so much fun making our way through it. Once we got done, we walked around, trying to find everyone. We came to a dance floor where people were dancing.

"Do you want to dance?"

"Oh, I don't know."

His parents danced to us, and his mom said, "Come on, the both of you!"

"We should do as she says before she gives us a tough time."

"Oh, fine." I sighed.

We stepped onto the dance floor. Nash took my hand and placed his hand on my lower back as he held me in a dance stance. The music played as he moved. I followed along with him, staring at my feet because I couldn't dance.

"Mags, look at me."

"I'm afraid I'll fall if I don't look at my feet."

"Do you trust me?"

I glanced at him.

"Trust me that I won't let you fall. Follow my lead."

I paid attention to Nash as he moved, following his lead. The minute I tripped, he caught me. He was right. He didn't let me fall. At that moment, I trusted Nash. I danced with him. He twirled me around and pulled me back to him.

Nash was a superb dancer. I smiled as he smiled. As we danced, his parents looked at us.

*****

Pat

"I told you," I told Nate.

"Okay, so they're cute together."

"Cute? Oh, Hunny. Maggie will be our future daughter-in-law."

"Patricia, not every person belongs together."

"True, but I trust my instincts. My instincts tell me that Nash and Maggie will end up together."

"If it happens, then it happens."

*****

Nixon

We walked up as Nash and Maggie danced.

"Interesting," Kat said.

"What?"

"Maggie doesn't dance."

"Well, she's dancing now."

"No, you don't understand. Maggie can't dance. She has two left feet," Marcy said.

We watched Nash and Maggie dance.

"For a girl with two left feet, she's doing a decent job," Noah said.

"Sometimes, you need the right partner to help you," Marcy said.

"What are you saying? Nash and Maggie?" Nathan asked. "No way."

"Is it unreasonable to believe that they're good together?" Kat asked.

Nash and Maggie danced, talked, and laughed.

"Don't Nash and Maggie deserve happiness?" Marcy asked us.

I sighed. "I guess."

"There's guessing. If two people belong together, it's those two. We'll give them the push they need," Kat said.

"You sound like Ma."

"That's an excellent complement." She smiled.

"No, it's creepy," Nathan said.

The girls and we conspired to get Nash and Maggie together. What could go wrong?

CHAPTER 15

MATCHMAKERS R US

Maggie

Here is a piece of advice. When matchmaking two people, try not to screw it up. If you're trying to play matchmaker, make sure you have their best interest at heart. I don't doubt the brothers had good intentions, but they needed a lesson in matchmaking.

We visited an apple orchard as a typical group outing. No biggie. That was when the expedition got screwy. The girls tried to make sure I ended up with Nash alone. So did the brothers. A small wrench got thrown into their plan like a random girl.

*****

Nixon

"Are we set?" Kat asked us.

"Yep, Nash will wait for her. He thinks he's waiting for us to show up," I said.

"Good, because we told her to meet us at the counter," Marcy said.

We stuck our heads around the corner and waited, watching with bated breath.

*****

Maggie

I walked up to the counter to find Nash there. "Hey, did you see the girls?"

"No, my idiot brothers were meeting me here."

"Oh, well, I hope they hurry."

We started talking, waiting for everyone to make their way to us, when a girl said, "Oh, my God, Nash!"

"Hey, Sarah."

The girl walked past me and hugged Nash. "Wow. You look great! How was Europe?"

"It was good."

I glanced around while they talked.

"Oh, Sarah. This is Maggie, who's staying with us."

Sarah and I shook hands.

"How do you know each other?" I asked her.

"Nash and I dated." She beamed.

"Oh."

"So, if you aren't busy, let's have dinner and catch up?"

Right, there was my cue to leave.

*****

Nixon

"What is that idiot doing?" Nathan asked.

"He's talking to another girl," Nolan said.

"Thank you, captain obvious," I said while rolling his eyes.

Maggie

I walked through the orchard. Why did I feel hurt? It's not like anything was happening between Nash and me. Was I expecting something to happen between us? I shook the thought from my head. He's a Gray brother, and the Gray Brothers don't like girls like me.

*****

Nash

"Dinner sounds great. Will Mike be there?"

"Well, duh. Mike is my fiancé." She rolled her eyes.

"Cool. I can't wait to catch up with Mike."

"Bring that girl with you."

"You mean Maggie?"

"Sure!"

"What do you say, Mags?" I noticed Mags gone. "Where did she go?"

"She was here a few minutes ago."

"I'll find her. Call me with the details, Sarah." I walked away from her and found Maggie reaching for an apple. I plucked it off the branch for her.

"Thanks." She rubbed the apple on her shirt.

"Why did you leave?"

"I figure you wanted to catch up." She shrugged.

"God, I haven't seen Sarah in the past year. It was great to see her again."

"So, dinner, huh?"

"Yeah, she wanted to catch up and said to bring you along."

"Oh, I don't want to intrude."

"It's dinner. Plus, you'd like Sarah."

"You should go and catch up."

"Are you okay?"

"I'm fine."

"No, you're not." I put my hands on my hips.

"Well, excuse me if I don't enjoy being the third wheel on your date." She moved her arms out.

"Date? What the hell? Maggie, you sound like a jealous girlfriend. The last time I checked, we're friends."

"Were."

"What?"

"We were friends."

Maggie walked away.

*****

Maggie

I found my friends.

"Hey, Mags," Kat said.

"Can we go?" I tried to stay calm in front of the brothers.

"Is something wrong?" Marcy asked.

"I want to leave without them." I pointed at the brothers. I didn't want to get stuck in a car with a Gray brother.

"Yeah, sure," Kat said.

We walked to Kat's car and left.

✶✶✶✶✶

Nash

I walked up to my brothers.

"Dude, what the hell?" Nixon asked.

"Got me. One minute, Maggie and I were talking. The next minute, she was acting like a jealous girlfriend."

"Who was the girl?" Noah asked me.

"What girl?"

"The one at the counter," Nathan said.

"That was Sarah."

"As in your ex?" Nixon asked.

"Yeah, she saw me and said hi. She asked me to have dinner with her and Mike, her fiancé. Said to bring Maggie. Then Maggie acted like a crazy nut."

"That explains so much." Nathan sighed.

"Huh?"

"Oh, God. You guys suck at this!" Nolan said. "You like her, and she likes you. She's jealous, and you're an idiot."

"What do you mean

He rolled his eyes. "You guys like each other. What part aren't you getting?"

"Nolan!" Nixon said.

"No, this whole matchmaking idea isn't working, so directness it is. Stop being a tool and ask Maggie out," Nolan told me.

"But she's Maggie."

"Yeah, so?" Nolan glanced at me.

"But she's Maggie."

"Yeah, we've proven she's Maggie, and you're Nash. Can we move on?" Nathan asked.

"Well, she's three years younger than me."

"So what? Dad is seven years older than Ma," Noah said.

"She's only seventeen."

"Yeah, then she'll be eighteen," Nixon said.

"And Maggie hates me."

"We can fix that," Noah said.

"How?"

"Well, I'm not sure, but we can," he said.

"Nash, you're finding every reason not to be with her. How about finding a reason to be with her?" Nixon asked.

I sighed and took a seat at the picnic table. "What if it fails?"

"What if it doesn't? You won't realize until you try," Nixon said.

"I'm not so sure." I hesitated, but my brothers didn't. If it was one thing about us that anyone understood, we took risks.

⁕⁕⁕⁕⁕

Maggie

I stormed past Pat and Nate. I was in no mood to talk. Jealous girlfriend? Ha! I'll give him a jealous girlfriend.

⁕⁕⁕⁕⁕

Pat

The boys came in a little while later. "So, will someone explain to me why Maggie is mad?" I asked.

The boys looked at their dad, who said, "You're on your own, boys." He raised his hands in defeat.

"I may or may not have called Maggie a jealous girlfriend," Nash said.

"Nash." I gave Nash a look that said you're lying, and I want the truth. If he doesn't tell me the truth, he better pray that someone finds his body because I'll kill him.

"Okay, fine. I called Maggie a jealous girlfriend."

"Why would you do that?"

"Because Numbnuts was talking to his ex, making dinner plans, and asked Maggie to tag along," Nixon said.

We gave him a look of disbelief.

"What?" Nash asked.

"Nash, you didn't," I said.

"Yes, I talked about dinner, but it included Mike, Sarah's fiancé. She mentioned bringing Maggie. Maggie didn't let me explain before she went off her nut and threw a hissy fit."

"Well, did you tell her?"

"Yes."

I arched a brow.

"No. I may have left out a few key details."

"A few key details? You made it sound like you had a date with another girl and asked Maggie to tag along," Nathan said.

"Well, son. I hate to say it, but you're an idiot," Nate said, walking by. "Am I wrong?"

"Nope, you're not wrong, Daddy-O," Nolan said.

"Nolan. Never call me that again."

"Yes, Dad."

"Well, now what do we do?" Nash asked.

"Do you like her?" I asked.

"Maybe." He shifted in his spot. "I mean, yeah."

"It's time to stop acting like a tool and show her, but it'll take some finesse."

"Thanks?" He arched an eyebrow at me.

"Well, don't be a tool." I shrugged, reminding him not to be an ass.

"Ma is outstanding." Noah smiled.

We conspired to get Nash and Maggie together.

CHAPTER 16

I LIKE YOU; YOU LIKE ME; WE'RE ONE BIG, HAPPY FAMILY

Maggie

Ever since the apple orchard, it's been tense between Nash and me. We came out of our bedrooms. I glared at him.

"After you," he said.

"Oh, no, after you."

"Oh, no. I insist."

"Fine."

"Fine."

"Great."

"Fantastic."

*****

Maggie

We faced each other at the breakfast table. The tension between us was palpable. No one said anything. Nixon sat next to Nash while I sat next to Noah.

"Nixon, pass me the syrup, please," I said even though the syrup was near Nash.

"Ask Nash since it's right by him." Nixon gestured at Nash while he ate.

"I don't want to ask Nash. I asked you," I spoke through gritted to him.

"Fine. Nash, pass Maggie the syrup," Nixon said.

I sat there, waiting.

Nash picked up the syrup bottle and tossed it to me, causing it to hit my plate and my plate to fall into my lap. "Oops." He snickered.

I let out a frustrated sigh, picked up my plate off my lap, and set it on the table. I scraped my pancakes off my lap and put them onto my plate.

"Noah, pass me the butter," Nash said.

"Ask Maggie," Noah said while continuing to eat.

"I asked you."

Noah shrugged. "Give Nash the butter, Maggie."

"Sure thing." I picked up the butter, threw it at Nash, and hit his chest. "Oops, I'm such a terrible shot." I smirked, enjoying the butter smacking him.

He cleaned the butter off him. That's all it took before we threw food at each other, causing the others to take cover or get out of the way.

We ceased fire. "You know what?" He leaned on the table with his palms.

"What?" I leaned on the table with my palms, coming face to face with him.

"You're a temperamental, little girl!"

"Well, you're a jerk!"

"And you're a brat!"

"Well, you're a tool!"

"Oh, yeah?"

"Yeah!"

"Well, this tool wants to kiss you!"

"Well, why don't you?"

He placed his hand on my head and pulled my lips to his as he kissed me, taking me by surprise. I tensed as he kissed me. Then I relaxed, wrapped my arms around his neck, and kissed him.

"Told ya," Pat told Nate.

Nate rolled his eyes.

He pulled back. "I like you."

"Well, I hate you."

"I don't care because I want to kiss you again." He pressed his lips to mine and kissed me again.

"You hate him, he likes you, and we're one big happy family. Thanks for ruining our breakfast, you twits," Nixon said.

We stop to glance at him.

Pat sent us upstairs to clean up while they cleaned up the kitchen. The brothers weren't happy about having to clean up our mess. Oh, well, they'll get over it. After taking a shower and changing my clothes, I came out of the bathroom.

Nash came out of his room. I waited for him to say something. He walked towards me as I fidgeted in my spot, then he walked past me. Well, okay, then. I headed downstairs to get more food. I started towards the table but changed my mind and went back upstairs. That kiss was a mistake.

*****

Pat

"Did I miss something?" Nate asked me.

"We all missed something." I glanced at Nash, who was busy eating his breakfast.

"Uh, Nash," Noah said, getting Nash's attention.

He looked up. "What?"

"Ma's giving you the stink eye," Nathan said.

"What?"

"My son is a tool." I rolled my eyes and shook her head.

*****

Maggie

I sat in my room, eating my breakfast. I thought about that kiss. Did Nash want to kiss me? Was it spontaneous? It's Nash Gray who would never have an interest in someone like me. None of the Grays would.

I'm the girl that got dumped on them by her parents. Since my parents left, I haven't heard from them — no phone calls, letters, or postcards. It's like they have forgotten about me. I sighed. And now I have a guy who says he likes me, kisses me, then acts like nothing ever happened. FML.

After finishing my breakfast, I took my plate to the kitchen and overheard Nate talking.

"Brian, please don't do this to her. Yes, we said we would take her. You said you would be back. You can't do this. She's your daughter. What do you mean, it's not your problem anymore?

Fine. You have a pleasant life, you selfish prick." He hung up his phone, then turned to see me. "Maggie." His expression was a mixture of anger towards my father and sympathy for me.

"That was my dad, wasn't it?" I figured I would go through the pleasantries.

"Yeah, he said that he and your mom are having a wonderful time and miss you." He tried to ease the painful truth.

"It's a lie. My parents don't miss me. If my parents did, they would have called me or sent a postcard. They're not coming back, are they?" I couldn't even face Nate. It was nice to learn that no one wants you.

"No. I'm sorry, Hunny. You'll stay here as long as you want."

"Thanks, Nate. Don't worry. After graduation, I'll find a place. It's a lot to take on another kid when you have five."

"Don't worry about it, Maggie. You're a part of our family. I'm sorry that you have a piece of shit for your parents."

"Yeah, I am too. My parents never wanted me, and I was a disruption to their lifestyle. It's funny. I grew up around money, but I wanted a family. It doesn't matter. I learned a long time ago that no one wants me. I'm someone to dump on other people."

*****

Nash

I stood by the doorway and listened to the whole exchange between my dad and Maggie. I winced and made a hasty retreat upstairs.

"Are you freaking kidding me?" Nixon asked.

"No. Dad was on the phone with him. Then Maggie overheard it."

"Dude, that's messed up," Noah said.

"Tell me about it." I sighed.

"Besides her having losers for parents, what about the elephant in the room you're avoiding?" Nathan asked.

"What elephant?"

"Not only did you tell Maggie that you liked her and kissed her, but now you're ignoring her," Nixon said.

"What if Maggie doesn't like me?"

"Dude, she kissed you! She likes you," Nathan said.

"Do you think so?"

"Oh, yeah," they said.

"Okay, now what?"

"Go tell her that you like her, you tool," Nolan said. "What? Do you disagree with my statement?"

"He has a point," Noah said.

"Okay, but if this blows up in my face, I'm kicking your asses."

"It won't. Now stop acting like a whining little bitch," Nixon said.

I opened Nixon's door and walked to Maggie's room. I knocked on the door, rubbing my palms on my pant legs.

Maggie opened the door. "Nash?"

I pulled her into a kiss. "I'm an idiot. I like you, Mags. I didn't think you would like me back. Say something because I'm dying."

"Okay."

"Huh?"

"Okay, I like you."

"Oh?" My face lit up.

"No."

My expression changed to sadness.

"I'm kidding." She grinned.

I rolled my eyes and pulled her into another kiss. "You're a funny girl," I spoke against her lips.

"Well, I live with funny boys." She shrugged. "Funny looking, that is."

"Oh, ha, ha."

She giggled.

"I like you, and you like me..."

Nixon interrupted us. "And we're one big freaking happy family! It isn't Barney. Ask her out already!"

"Damn, Nixon."

Mags snickered.

I turned to face her. "Will you go out on a date with me?"

"Yes." She smiled.

"Great." I backed away, trying to act nonchalant.

"Great."

"Outstanding."

I walked out of the room, then realized I never said when. Well, shit. I popped my head in the doorway. "A day and time would work."

"Yep."

"How about tomorrow night around five?"

"Five would be good."

"Great, I'll see you then."

I left, leaving Mags perplexed.

CHAPTER 17

FIRST DATE MISHAPS

Maggie

I still couldn't believe I was going on a date with Nash. It was weird. I grew up next to him my entire life. He and his brothers used to run over my barbies with their remote-control cars. Now I'm going on a date with him. He was my first kiss. The infamous food fight in the kitchen was when I had my first kiss. I had no clue what I was doing when it happened.

I finished getting ready as Nate gave Nash ground rules.

*****

Nash

"There's no improper touching, roaming hands, or pressure."

"Shouldn't a father encourage their sons to do nasty things with a girl?"

"Yeah, for the most part. It's the first time I'm acting like a father figure to a teen girl." He sat next to me. "I have to tell you, son. It isn't easy to juggle two different kids. I want to give you advice, but I want to protect Maggie."

"It sucks, doesn't it?"

"You have no idea." Dad waved his hand in the air with an expression of helplessness.

Pat

I helped Maggie get ready, and when we finished, we came downstairs. Nash and Nate both stood. "Any advice?" Maggie asked me.

"Yeah, don't get pregnant."

She gave her a weird expression, then walked over to Nash, and they left for their date.

"Well, that went well," Nate said.

Maggie

We walked to the car.

"What was with a weird face?" Nash asked me.

I opened my car door. "I asked your mom for advice."

"And?"

"She said don't get pregnant."

He chuckled as we got into the car. Nash drove to a diner. We hurried inside to find a booth, then scanned the menu.

"You gotta be kidding me?" Bryson stood there. "Can't you eat somewhere else?"

"Well, this place is cheap, and we're hungry? So, no," Nash said.

"What if I don't want to serve you?"

"Then you can get us a manager, you tool." Nash smirked.

"Whatever. What do you want?"

"I'll have a burger, fries, and a chocolate milkshake," I said.

"That sounds good. I'll have the same," Nash said.

"Fine. I'll be right back," Bryson said.

"Oh, and Bryson." Nash stopped him. "Don't even think about spitting in our food or anything else you have planned, or I'll beat the shit out of you."

Bryson's shoulders slumped as he made his way to the kitchen. I chuckled.

Once our food arrived, we talked while eating. Nash and I had a lot in common with similar tastes. It ranged from movies to books to music. He spoke about what it was like to backpack through Europe. He made me smile. We talked about stuff we did as kids. Our childhood was funny.

After we ate, we headed to the movies. I took it easy on Nash and picked an action movie. We found our seats, and I played with the armrest buttons, moving my seat.

"What are you doing?"

"I'm pretending to be Sully from Monsters, Inc." I grinned.

He chuckled. "Okay, it's cute."

"Come to the dark side. We have cookies." I smirked as Nash roared.

"Will you shut up?" Someone asked.

Nash glimpsed over his chair's back. "Nathan, I'll beat your ass!"

"Dude, chill. It was a joke!"

I glanced over my seat's back. "Are you serious? Was it crucial for the four of you to follow us?"

"Blame, Dad. He didn't want you both to do anything improper. Enjoy making out!" Noah said.

"And Ma doesn't want Nash to knock you up!" Nixon said.

I lowered my face into the back of the seat. Why me? Oh, that's right. I agreed to a date with one of the Gray brothers. It meant going out with each brother.

"They can make out. Free porn!" Nolan said.

"Nolan, you're such a perv!" Nixon said.

Noah hauled off and smacked Nolan on the back of his head.

"Welcome to the family, Mags."

I arched an eyebrow and groaned. Welcome to the family, indeed.

*****

We snuck out of the movie theater before the boys caught us, and Nash drove us to a secluded spot. I looked around and then at him. "You won't kill me, will you?"

"What? No. You've been watching too many movies." He rolled his eyes.

"Okay, then you won't try to knock me up, will you?"

"Sure, and have my parents kill me. No, thanks."

"Then what will you do?"

"This." He pulled me to him and kissed me. We kissed for a while, then he stopped.

"Did I do something wrong?"

"No."

"I did. I'm a terrible kisser." I sighed.

"What? No. You're a fantastic kisser."

"Then why did you stop kissing me?"

Don't judge. You were thinking the same thing.

"Because I need to ask you a crucial question."

"You won't propose, will you? Because, well, it's our first date. That would be sudden."

He rolled his eyes at my foolish statement. "Mags, we need to be a couple before that happens."

"What?" Then I realized what he meant. "Are you asking me to be your girlfriend?"

"Well, do you accept?"

My eyes widened. "You want me to be your girlfriend."

"Well, that's what a couple means."

"What about the girl at the apple orchard?"

"Sarah?"

"Yeah."

"Sarah is my ex and engaged to a buddy of mine."

"Oh." Now I felt like a tool.

"FYI, jealousy is an excellent look on you. Your nose scrunches up, and you get these short lines right here." Nash pointed to a space between his brows. I laughed as he smiled at me.

"You were my first kiss."

His brows raised. "Oh?"

"Hello! For four years, I had pined for a tool."

He chuckled. "Well, I hope I'm your first and last kiss."

My cheeks heated, and I covered my cheeks.

He pulled my hands from my cheeks. "Don't. I love it when you blush." That made me blush more as he smiled.

Then someone tapped on the window. Nash unrolled the window as a light flashed in his face.

"Excuse us, sir. You're in an unauthorized section," a deep voice said.

"What?" He squinted at the person.

"You're in a place you shouldn't be, you tool. Damn, you're dumb."

He gripped the steering wheel. "Nix, I'll kill you if you don't get that damn light off me."

He turned it off and leaned in. "Did you ask Maggie?"

Nash glanced at him. "What do you think?"

"Did she say yes?" Noah asked him.

Nash looked at me. "Did you say yes?"

"Yep," I said.

He turned to them. "Mags said yes."

"You didn't knock her up, did you?" Nathan asked him.

"I have no words for you," Nash said.

"I'm just checking." Nathan smirked.

"So, does this mean I can't steal her bras anymore?" Nolan asked him.

"Nolan, when did you ever steal her bra?" Nash asked him.

"Never mind. I said nothing," Nolan said.

He glanced at me, and I said, "I'll fill you in later."

"I missed a lot while I was gone."

"More than you know." I giggled.

"Now, if you idiots don't mind, I'm taking my girl home," he said.

The brothers stepped back while he started the car and pulled out of the spot.

*****

Nixon

"Do you know what this means?" Nathan asked.

"Oh, yeah," they said. "Fresh meat."

"Nash will kill us." Noah sighed.

"Eh, he'll get over it," Nixon said.

"This should be good." Nathan rubbed his hands together.

Yep, we had plans for Nash and Maggie and wanted to have our fun. Except we weren't aware that we met our match with Maggie.

CHAPTER 18

BLUE BALLS

Maggie

After our date, Nash and I hung out more. We threw in kissing here and there, but we kept it PG and simple. It's easier than dealing with prying eyes, aka the brothers.

Nash and I enjoyed our new couplehood. Nathan had issues with Macey as he got rambunctious with her.

*****

Nathan

When things got intense, I was in Macey's room, making out with her. As we kept kissing, I undid my pants, finding relief as my pants had tightened. Then it happened. I let out a groan against her lips as I released myself onto her.

"What the hell, Nathan?"

My eyes popped open. Then I saw the white, milky substance on Macey, and I turned pink. I buttoned my pants and bolted out of there. While I took off for home, Noah was busy with Marcy.

*****

Noah

I was on Marcy's bed as she gave me pleasure with her mouth. I was finding my release when Marcy stopped. She heard the exchange through the door with Macey yelling. Then doors slammed.

I propped myself. "Baby, why did you stop? I was almost there."

"Save it, Noah. Something happened between my sister and your brother."

"What? Are your twin senses tingling?"

"No, but you're an idiot." She smacked me and rolled her eyes. Then she stood up. "Get up. You should leave."

"What? Why?"

"I need to talk to my sister."

I grumbled and buttoned my pants. The tightness from not having a release became agonizing. I crept towards the door and headed home.

The next issue was one for the books.

*****

Maggie

I was in my room working on homework. Nash was in the kitchen making something to eat. The door opened and slammed shut. He walked to the doorway as Nathan stomped up the steps. Noah followed behind with a painful stroll.

That wasn't good. Nash followed the demon twins up to their rooms.

I opened my door when someone slammed theirs. Noah hobbled to his room as Nash reached the top of the steps. Then Noah screamed. Nathan's door opened, and we rushed to Noah's room.

Nash opened the door to find Noah trying to undo his pants, but every time he tried, he screamed and stopped.

"What the hell?" I asked.

"Noah?" Nash asked.

"Yes?"

"What's wrong?"

"Oh, nothing."

"Noah."

"I'm good, Nash. I need to get my pants off." He tried not to scream.

Nathan covered his face with his hand.

"Nathan?" Nash asked.

He peeked through his hand. "Blue balls."

"What?"

We looked at him, unsure of what he said.

He pulled his hand away and gestured at Noah. "He has blue balls, okay?"

"On that note, I'm out of here," I said.

*****

Nash

I shook my head and turned to Noah. "How the hell did you get blue balls?"

"Well, Marcy went down on me when Macey yelled. Marcy stopped. She made me go home." Noah glared at Nathan. "What did you do?"

"What do you mean?"

"Come on, Nathan. You did something. What was it?"

"What did you do?" I asked Nathan.

"Fine. Macey and I were making out. I undid my pants, not wanting to feel the pressure. Then, I ended up shooting my load." We both stared at him as he said, "On her."

We did a double-take as Nathan fidgeted in his spot. Then it happened. I roared with laughter.

"This isn't funny, Nash!" Nathan said.

"Yes, it is." He snickered.

"I'm glad you find this funny, but having blue balls isn't!"

"Okay, that isn't funny. What you did was funny." I earned a glare from Nathan.

"What should I do?" Nathan asked.

"Little brother, if you're not going to get any, you take care of business ahead of time. You learn to control your shit."

"That's easier said than done when you have done nothing." Nathan sat on Noah's bed.

I took a seat next to him. "Being a virgin isn't terrible, but you haven't learned proper control."

"How did you learn?"

"It helps to think of something that turns you off."

"Is that what you do?"

"Yeah, or I handle my business if you catch my drift."

"I'm glad you two are bonding, but I need help here," Noah said.

We helped Noah with his pants. Noah shoved them down and walked to his bed.

"I'll be back with some ice." I left the room.

"Yeah, you're on your own, dude," Nathan said, leaving the room.

While Noah dealt with his blue balls, I got an ice pack for him when Nixon came into the kitchen.

"Where have you been?"

"Hanging with Kat. Why?"

"Because yin and yang got themselves into a mess."

Nixon looked at the ice pack. "Someone has blue balls."

"Yep."

"Nathan?"

"Nope."

Nixon's brows raised. "Noah?"

"Well, Nathan shot early with Macey. Marcy gave Noah head then stopped, not letting him finish."

"Damn, that's harsh."

"You know what this means, don't you?"

"Psh, they didn't think we'd let this slide?"

"Well, if they do, they're dumb."

Nixon laughed. If you're wondering, we'll make jokes at the twins' expense. That is a fact between brothers. If we find something embarrassing about you and can use it against you, we will.

*****

Maggie

Nash tended to Noah.

Nixon said, "Damn, boys. Blue balls and a minute man aren't a beautiful attribute!"

"Screw you, Nix!" Nathan said.

"Piss off, Nix!" Noah said.

Nash came into my bedroom and sat on my bed.

"Well, the boys aren't having a pleasant day," I said.

"Pleasant day? Nope, more like they'll regret it." He chuckled.

"Is it nice to make fun of them?"

"Did you not learn anything from living with us? We never said we're nice. It's a rule to make fun of each other."

I chuckled. The Gray brothers are infamous for finding something embarrassing about you and running with it. I have been on the receiving end.

Then Nolan said, "Blue balls? You're a sad, sad man, Noah!"

"Nolan, I'll beat your ass if you don't shut the hell up!"

"Eh, you'll have to catch me, but you can't have blue balls first."

"I have an idea if you're up for it," Nash said.

What did he have planned?

"But first, I need Nix's input."

That isn't good. When Nash comes up with an idea, it results in something happening. I'm so in.

"What's your idea?"

"Well, first things first." He leaned over and kissed me. I wrapped my arms around his neck and kissed him back. He pulled me onto his lap, making out with me. Then he stopped. "Okay, no offense. I don't need blue balls myself."

I laughed as he gave me a quick peck on the lips and moved me off his lap.

"Let's go." He took my hand and led me out of the room.

Okay, I should explain blue balls. I learned about it from my friends since I knew little about guys. Dad is never around, and I don't have brothers. I grew up next to the brothers.

Blue balls are when a guy doesn't end up having an orgasm and releasing himself. His balls become engorged, and it's highly uncomfortable. A guy's balls have a blue hint to them. They're usually purple and darker than the rest of the body. I never saw a guy's balls or any other part of them, only what I had learned in health class or from my friends.

It's all new to me. Trust me. I would encounter more stuff living with the Gray brothers. It's more than I wanted to know.

CHAPTER 19

BLUE LIPS

Maggie

Nash, Nixon, and I stood in the local grocery store's bakery section in front of glass cases.

"A cake?" I asked.

"Yep," they both said.

"Why a cake?" I was confused with the whole theory of getting a cake for something like blue balls until they explained it.

"Because we must mourn what one has lost, and we love cake." Nixon raised a finger, emphasizing his point.

They searched through the case until they found one with blue icing.

"Perfect." Nash pulled out a cake without writing. A genius can figure out why he picked this cake.

He took the cake to the baker, whispering to him. The baker shrugged, taking the cake to the back.

"What did you say to him?" I asked him.

"You'll see." He shot Nixon a knowing expression.

Once Nash paid for the cake, we returned to the house. Pat and Nate read the cake as they rolled their eyes. Noah likes to dish out the jokes, but he doesn't want to take them.

The boys made their way to Noah's room. They walked inside with the cake. Noah glanced at the writing: Here Lies Noah's Balls, May They Rest in Peace.

He nodded. "Cute, guys."

"Yeah, we thought so." Nash smirked.

"You guys are tools."

"It's funny." Nixon snickered.

"Funny? That's hilarious!" Nolan said.

They laughed while Noah got pissed. I giggled when he zeroed in on me.

"You think the joke is funny?" He shot me a glare.

"Well, yeah." I giggled some more.

"I'm glad you think it's funny since your friend gave me blue balls!"

"Whoa. Wait. I had nothing to do with what had happened."

"Oh, because we had nothing but problems since you got here."

"Noah, hey, man. Come on," Nixon said, trying to diffuse the situation.

"No." He snapped his face towards Nixon. "She doesn't belong here. Her parents dumped her on us because they don't give a shit." He turned back to me. "Now, I know why."

It was too late. I stood there, shocked, and stared at Noah. I have never felt so hurt. Noah's outburst left the boys speechless. I walked out of the room. My parents dumped me and didn't care. Why stay where I'm not wanted?

*****

Nash

I walked over to Noah. "That was a dick move."

He pointed at the cake. "Like this wasn't?"

"The cake was mine and Nix's idea. Maggie had nothing to do with the cake. If you want to get pissed, then get pissed at us." I left Noah's room and went to Mag's room. I knocked on the door. "Mags?" She didn't respond. I opened the door and found her packing. "What are you doing?"

"I'm packing. I'm a burden and unwanted." She wouldn't even face me.

"Maggie, he didn't mean what he said. He's mad."

"Yeah, like my parents didn't mean to leave me with no intention of coming back. It's okay. I realized I'm not wanted." She picked up items and shoved them into her bag.

I walked over and touched her. She fought me, but I pulled her to me.

"Why doesn't anyone want me, Nash? What did I do wrong?"

"Hun, I don't know. I want you, and so does my family."

"But Noah." She sniffled.

"Noah is a tool, and his opinion doesn't mean shit right now."

She buried her face into me. "But I want someone to want me. I have no home, no family, and no one."

"Well, you have me."

She looked up at me with tear-streaked cheeks.

"And you have us." She turned and glimpsed at the rest of my family, minus Noah.

Dad and Ma entered the room.

"Maggie, we know living here has been a rough change, but it's been worth having you here. You're family to us," Dad said.

"But Noah." She sniffled.

"Don't worry about Noah. I'll take care of him. You're welcome here if you like. Isn't that right, boys?"

"Yes," we said.

"I didn't get that."

"Yes." We plastered a smile on our faces.

"Now, excuse me. I have a matter with ole blue balls himself." Dad left the room. I put his hand up to stop Mags from saying anything else.

Then we heard yelling from Noah's room. We hurried to the door to listen.

"But Dad!" Noah said.

"I don't give a shit, Noah! You had no right to say those words! She didn't tell her friend to give you a blowjob and stop the last time I checked!"

"Can we not talk about it?"

"Who cares? So, you got one and ended up with blue balls. Blue balls happen to the best of us."

"This is embarrassing."

"Yeah, well, it's about to get worse. Maggie is a permanent guest in this house. If you or your yahoo brothers cause her to leave, I'll cut off your dicks. Do I make myself clear?"

We covered their manhood. "Crystal."

"Good. Now, let's have some cake." Dad carried the cake out of Noah's room. "Who wants cake?"

We raised our hands. You didn't have to ask us twice.

*****

Maggie

As we ate cake, Nixon said, "You look like you blew a Smurf."
He laughed, as did everyone else.

"So do the rest of you." I shrugged, causing them to shut up.
Don't joke when you appear guilty.

As I ate my cake, Noah tried to talk to me. "Maggie?"

I glanced at him.

"I'm..."

I cut him off. "Save it. You made your feelings clear about me.
So, let's call it a day." I walked away. I wouldn't let him off the
hook. His words hurt, and an apology won't make the situation
better.

He sighed. His brothers looked away. "This is a fantastic
cake," Nixon said.

"The best," Nash said.

"A little help here," Noah said.

"Sorry, brother, but you're on your own." Nathan took a bite
of the cake.

"Not going to happen," Nolan said.

"Ma?"

"Coffee sounds great, Nate," she said.

"You're right. Bye," Nate told Noah, then followed Pat into the
kitchen.

"Thanks for the help, guys!"

The brothers shrugged. Noah would need to apologize to me without help from his brothers. He needed to learn to keep his temper in check.

I was in the kitchen with Pat and Nate. Noah walked over to me. "Maggie?"

I shot him a glance.

"Please, hear me out." Then he glanced at his parents. "Do you mind?"

"No, by all means, go ahead," his mom said while drinking her coffee.

He rolled his eyes. "I'm sorry. I didn't mean what I said. I was angry, but it's no excuse."

"No, it's not. Noah, do you think I enjoy getting dumped on people? I've had that done to me my entire life. Your parents don't want you because you're in the way of their freedom. It sucks, but you deal with it."

"I messed up, but please, please forgive me."

"Beg."

"You're not serious."

"Yep, I am. Now, beg." I pointed to the floor.

He huffed and got on his knees. "I beg you to forgive me. Please, please, please forgive me."

The boys watched, as did Pat and Nate. Noah was on his knees, begging for my forgiveness.

"Do you forgive me?"

"Let me check." I tapped my finger against my chin. "No."

He stood up. "What?"

A smirk grew upon my face. "I'm kidding."

"Huh?"

"Yo, tool, she forgave you," Nathan said from the doorway.

Everyone grinned, then he turned back to me. "Well played, grasshopper."

I shrugged. "Well, I learned from you boys."

He kissed me on the cheek and walked out of the kitchen. Nash glanced at me as I shrugged.

"Our boys met their match," Nate told Pat.

"You owe me five bucks." She held out her palm to him.

He pulled a five out of his jean pocket and slapped it into her palm. "Remind me never to bet against you again."

"Yeah, sure. Didn't you learn anything from when we were kids?"

"That you're a sneaky little thing? Yep." He sipped his coffee.

She gave him a playful smack while rolling her eyes.

I love Pat and Nate. They're awesome.

CHAPTER 20

SCARE FEST WITH THE GRAYS: A HALLOWEEN CHAPTER

Maggie

Do you know what's scarier than horror movies and ghosts on Halloween? It's Halloween with the Grays. They go all out for it since it's their favorite holiday in the world. They love to scare people.

As a kid, I went trick or treating. They would always scare me. Yeah, I hated them for scaring me. They laughed, and I cried. It was a fun time.

This year, besides setting up decorations for Halloween, we're going to a costume party at Kat's house. The girls and I shopped for a costume. As we were trying on outfits, they were discussing the brothers.

"He did what?" Kat stuck her head out of the curtain's opening in the changing room.

"He jizzed on me," Macey said.

"Why?"

"Who knows? The dude can't hold it together for longer than two minutes."

"The twins are virgins," I said, letting the information slip.

"What?" The girls asked.

I popped my head out through the curtain's opening of the changing room. "The twins are virgins. They've never had sex."

"We understand what virgins mean, stoop," Macey said.

"That's why Nathan didn't last."

"What about Nixon, Kat?" Marcy asked.

"What about him?"

"Have you guys done anything?"

"What do you think?" Kat walked out of the changing room, looking in the mirror at her costume.

"What?"

"Yeah, we did."

"How was it?"

"It was okay. Nothing like I expected."

"What did you expect?" I walked out of the changing room in my costume.

"Something like the movies. It was awkward. I don't think Nixon has any sexual experience," she said. "Come on, Maggie."

"Come on, what?"

"You live with them. Did Nixon go out with many girls?" Macey asked.

"How should I know? I live with them. It's not like I know their sexual needs."

"Well, you know the twins are virgins," Marcy said.

"Only because Nash told me. Why are we talking about this? Let's get our costumes and go." I stepped back into the changing room, changing into my regular clothes. I didn't want to discuss sex and the Gray brothers.

Once we changed, we left. We didn't realize we had company in the changing rooms with us. As soon as we left, Tiffany stepped out. She made a call. "Bryson? Change of plans. We are going to a Halloween party tonight. I'll fill you in when I get to your house. Love you. Bye."

*****

The boys and I got ready for the party as Nate and Pat handed out candy. I came out of my room.

"Well, you're a cute little devil."

"Yeah, I had a tough time deciding between a cat, devil, or fairy."

"Well, you look good in anything." He smiled.

I rolled my eyes. "You're such a charmer."

"I try." He smirked as we came downstairs.

We made our way to the party. Once we got there, we made our way inside. The boys searched for the girls. Nolan looked for any girl who moved and was alone. Nash and I hung out in the kitchen, having a drink.

We were having a fun time until two unexpected party crashers arrived. Tiffany filled in Bryson about our conversation in the changing rooms. They put their plan into action. Operation ruined Maggie's night.

Bryson and Tiffany split up. They told each person personal things about the brothers' lack of sexual experience. Tiffany had listened in on the conversation in the dressing room. Word traveled fast and got back to the brothers. They ended up fighting with the girls.

Nolan ran into the kitchen, pulled Nash towards him, and whispered what he heard.

"What?" Nash's jaw clenched.

"Nash, it's all over the party."

They glanced at me.

"What?"

"Did you say anything about the twins?"

"No. Why?"

"Don't lie to me, Maggie."

"I'm not lying!"

"Then how would everyone know about them not having any sexual experience? The only ones that knew were my brothers, you, and your friends."

"Okay, fine. We were in the changing room. The girls mentioned what happened to them and your brothers. I said something to them to help them understand."

"It wasn't your call, Maggie."

"I'm sorry."

"Sorry, won't cut it. Now I have to fix this mess that you created."

Nixon stormed past Nash.

Nash caught his arm. "Where are you going?"

"Ask your girlfriend and her friends. I'm lousy in bed! Oh, let me rephrase that. I'm awkward." He stormed out.

Nash got the twins, along with Nolan, and left.

I ran after them. "Nash!"

He stopped and turned to face me. "Don't. You've done enough." He got into the car.

They left me standing alone. I turned around to see my friends glaring at me. They turned to go back inside.

I walked up to Kat. "Kat?"

"Go, Maggie." She went back inside, leaving me feeling abandoned again.

I didn't even understand what I had done. One minute, I was having fun, and the next, I was standing outside alone. As I stood there, Bryson and Tiffany walked up.

"Man, that sucks. I guess things don't work out for the best. Oh, wait, for us, they did. You have a pleasant night," Bryson said.

They walked by laughing.

I walked back to the Gray house and saw Nate and Pat sitting outside on the front porch with a candy bowl. I sighed and walked up.

"Is the party over so soon?" Nate asked me.

"Something like that. Did the boys come home?"

"Yeah, a few minutes ago. They're up in their rooms. They said that they're tired," Pat said.

"Oh, well, I'll tell you."

"Tell us what, sweetheart?" Nate asked.

I told them the truth. Nate and Pat treated me well. They deserved to know what had happened at the party. They listened to me.

"Don't be mad at the boys. It was my fault. I promise to make myself scarce, so the brothers won't have to see me. I don't want to cause problems." I walked past them.

"Maggie?" Nate stopped me and gave me a soft smile.

"Yeah?"

"Thanks for telling us."

"Sure."

I walked upstairs and removed my horns. I walked to Nash's door and placed my palm on it. "I'm sorry, Nash." I turned, going into my room. I changed out of my costume and into something comfy. I needed a place to stay. I'm grateful that Nate and Pat let me stay here, but my presence was causing too many issues.

*****

The next day, I stayed in my room except for school. At school, everyone ignored me. I don't blame them. I would have ignored me, too. Bryson and Tiffany got what they wanted.

When I got home, I hurried past Nash, going up to my room. He hated me, and so did the others. The best thing I could do was make myself scarce. At dinner, I came down while everyone ate at the table. I grabbed something small, taking it to my room. I didn't want them to think I was taking more from them than I did. I broke their trust.

*****

Pat

"We should take Maggie out for ice cream to cheer her up," Nate said.

"That's a superb idea," I said.

"Why?" Nixon asked.

"Why not?" Nate asked.

"It's not like she deserves it," Nathan said.

"Huh, you're right. Then again, Maggie doesn't deserve the treatment she is getting. I don't know, Pat. What do you think?" Nate glanced at me.

"Well, Nate, she made a simple mistake and wasn't aware she had listening ears. But that is none of my business." I took a bite of my food.

"What do you mean?" Nash asked me.

"Nothing. It's not like the gossip started from Maggie's mouth or anything. She got the blame because someone else caused trouble. But again, that is none of my business."

"What do you mean, someone else?" Noah asked her.

"Someone else was the one that started everything, you dolt," Nolan said. "Damn, you're slow."

The boys glanced at him.

"Am I wrong? No, I'm not."

Nate and I glanced at each other. We gave each other a knowing smile, then started eating. It takes one little birdie to whisper something in one's ear.

*****

Maggie

After dinner, Pat and Nate took me out for ice cream. Thank God we were inside because it was November, and it was getting cold. They sat across from me in the booth as I jabbed my sundae.

"Maggie, how's your ice cream?" Nate ate his ice cream.

I shrugged and picked at it with my spoon.

"So, someone has an upcoming birthday," Pat told Nate.

"Oh, yeah? Do tell."

"Someone special is turning eighteen, isn't that right, Maggie?"

I stared at them. "Um, yeah, I guess."

"Well, I thought we could have cake, ice cream, pizza, and rent two movies. Doesn't that sound like fun?"

I wasn't happy to celebrate anything, let alone my birthday.

"That sounds boring," a voice said.

We saw the brothers.

"Who says that I'm inviting you?" She asked. "I'm planning this, not you, so go away."

"Well, you suck at planning parties," Nixon said.

"I beg your pardon. Did I ask for your opinion? No. Now, return to your sulking."

"No offense, Ma, but no girl wants movies and pizza for her eighteenth birthday," Noah said.

"How would you know? Were you ever an eighteen-year-old girl? No, so your opinion is invalid. Plus, shouldn't you pout about your sexual exploits? Oh, please. I'm your mother, not stupid. And whatever issue you boys have are your issues, not hers, so stop being tools."

"Well said, Hun," Nate said.

"I thought so."

I love Nate and Pat. They're fantastic.

Nash took a seat next to me. "We're sorry. Saying it won't change what happened, but you didn't deserve to get iced out."

I didn't know what to say. The minute I opened my mouth, the shit hit the fan.

"Say something, Maggie."

I sighed, then picked up my dessert and smashed it into his face.

It fell into his lap. "Guess I deserved that."

I wouldn't let him off the hook with an apology. I gauged what he would do. He sat there for a minute, tapping his fingertips on the table. He grabbed my face and gave me a big ole sloppy ice cream kiss. I laughed, as he did, too. He wiped off the ice cream and flicked it at me.

What will I do with these boys?

CHAPTER 21

DRUNKEN ANTICS

Nash

After discovering that Bryson and Tiffany caused the mess, I visited Bryson. I leaned against the wall when Bryson came strolling out of a store.

"That was a neat little stunt you pulled back there on Halloween, trying to embarrass my brothers. Then letting Maggie take the fall." My deep voice caught Bryson off guard.

Bryson stopped. "I don't know what you mean."

I stood up and walked over to him. "You don't know what I mean, you tool. How dumb do you think I am?"

"Well…"

"It's funny. I don't know what Mags saw in you. You're a weasel who prefers to humiliate others to make themselves feel better."

"What are you going to do? Beat me up."

"Nope. I'll let big brother handle you." I pointed at Mike, Bryson's older brother and Sarah's fiancé.

"Bryson, you little shit! Why are you giving this poor girl a tough time?"

"Come on, Mike."

"Don't come on, me. That was low, even for you. Now get home. Mom and Dad want a word with you."

Bryson walked away in a huff.

"Damn, kids. They assume they know more than us," Mike said.

"Tell me about it."

"Hey, Sarah still wants to have dinner."

"Tell Sarah sometime next week. I'll talk to Mags about it."

"Sounds good. Don't forget. You're getting an invitation to the wedding." Mike walked away.

"Can't wait!"

*****

Maggie

I was lying on my bed, reading when Nash plopped next to me.

"Where were you?" I looked up from my book.

"I had business to take care of with Nix. What are you doing?"

I held up the book. "Reading."

"Well, I can figure out better things to do." He crawled over to me, pulling me to him. The brothers shouted in the hallway.

"What are those yahoos yelling about now?"

"Your brothers have been yelling the entire day."

He opened the door to find his brothers arguing.

"You're not going, Nolan!" Nixon said.

"Why not?"

"Because it's a high school party!"

"Yeah, and I'm in high school. What's your point?"

"Because none of us are going, that's my point!"

"Well, you're not in charge!"

"Listen, dipwad. You're not going," Nathan said.

"Who will stop me?"

"He will." Noah pointed at Nash, who stood next to Nixon.

"Come on, Nash," Nolan said.

"Ma and Dad left me in charge while they're away. No one is going to any parties. Period," Nash said.

"Fine! Can I go to Charlie's house?"

"As long as it's Charlie's house and not a party. Trust me. I'll check on you."

"It'll be Charlie's." Nolan went to call his friend Charlie.

*****

Nolan

A little while later, Nash dropped me off at Charlie's. He leaned over the seat. "Remember, what I said, Nolan."

"Yeah, yeah, yeah." I walked away from the car. Nash pulled out, and I walked inside and up to Charlie's room.

"Well?" Charlie asked.

"They suspect nothing. We're going to that party. My brothers can't stop me."

"Right on, man." Charlie gave me a slap handshake.

*****

Charlie and I arrived at the booming party. People were dancing, laughing, and drinking. We walked around until they found a punch bowl. I picked up a glass.

"What if it's spiked?" Charlie asked me.

"Who would spike the punch? I'm sure it's for people who don't drink."

"I'll stick to pop."

"Suit yourself." I filled a cup to the brim. "Bottoms up, Charlie." With that, I started drinking, drinking, and drinking more punch.

After about three cups of punch, I became lit. Someone had spiked the punch. I staggered around, looking for Charlie until I found him. "Charlie, there you are!"

"Are you drunk?"

"Nah, it's punch. *Hic.* It would be best if you tried it." I was slurring my words.

"No, thanks. I'll pass."

"Well, I'm getting more." I staggered towards the punch bowl. As the night progressed, so did my drunken antics, causing Charlie to worry.

"Nolan! Come on! Get down from there!"

I stood on top of a table while drinking and dancing. After enough coaxing, Charlie got me down, and I swayed.

"Great, your brothers will kill us." He tried to help me.

"Oh, no! Nash will kill me!" My eyes widened.

"I need to call someone. If I call my mom, she'll call yours."

"No. You can't call my Ma. She'll kill me."

"Okay, then I'll call one of your brothers."

"No, you can't call them either."

"Then, who?"

I pondered for a minute while swaying back. "I got it. Call Maddie."

"Who's Maddie?"

"The girl who lives with us and loves Nash. You know, Maddie."

Charlie took a deep breath and pulled out my phone, searching through the names. "Well, it's not Maddie, but it's close enough." He dialed the number.

Nolan?

"It's Charlie. Is this Maddie?"

No, It's Maggie.

"The girl that lives with Nolan and loves Nash?"

Yes. The jury is still out on Nash. Where's Nolan?

"Can you not be anywhere near his brothers right now?"

Yeah, hang on. I'm going to the kitchen! No, get your own sandwich! Well, I'm not your mother! I'm sorry about that. Nash is such a baby. What's up?

"It's Nolan."

What about Nolan?

"Well, he's." Charlie turned to see me staggering around and falling.

He's what?

There was silence.

He's what, Charlie?

I got to my feet and started stripping.

"He's drunk but don't tell his brothers."

Okay.

"Can you come and get us?"

I don't have my license.

"What senior doesn't have their license?"

This senior doesn't. Let me make a call. Text me the address. I'll come and get both of you.

"Thanks, Maggie."

*****

Maggie

I walked into the living room, where the brothers were sitting.

"Is everything okay?" Nash asked me.

"Um, yes. That was Kat. She needs help."

"With what?" Nixon asked.

"With that time of the month. Yep. Kat needs help with buying tampons."

"Ew, gross." The brothers groaned.

"I'll be back after helping her buy tampons. Bye." I left and walked, meeting Kat down the street. I climbed into her car.

"Why am I helping you again?"

"Because you owe me for Halloween."

"Fine." She sighed.

We drove until we found the house. She parked out front, and we both got out of the car.

"Maddie!" Nolan said.

Nolan was drunk as a skunk, with Charlie trying to hold him up. We walked over to them.

"Isn't your name Maggie?" Charlie asked me.

"Yes." I took Nolan from Charlie with Kat's help, and we helped him to the car with Charlie following behind us. Once we were inside, we dropped Charlie off at his home, then drove back to the house.

We pulled in, and Kat turned off the car. We both glanced at Nolan. He was three sheets to the wind.

Nolan waved at us. "Hey, guys."

"How are we going to get Nolan past his brothers?"

"With a wish and a prayer. Let's hope Nolan doesn't puke on us." I cringed.

We got out of the car, dragging him out of the backseat. "For a smaller guy than his brothers, he sure weighs a ton."

"Tell me about it."

We got to the kitchen door, leaning Nolan against the house. "You be quiet, Nolan." I put my finger on my lips.

"Shh." He mimicked me with his fingers while laughing.

"Good boy. We'll go in, so your brothers miss us."

"That would be terrible!" His eyes widened.

"Yes, it would be."

We got him inside and helped Nolan up the stairs until a light turned on.

Nash asked, "Maggie?"

I stuck my head around the corner. "Oh, hey, Nash."

"What's happening?"

That's when it happened.

"Nash! Hey!"

Nolan tumbled down the steps. Kat and I facepalmed ourselves as Nolan fell right on his face.

CHAPTER 22

DRUNKEN ANTICS, PART TWO

Maggie

The other brothers came into the kitchen. They found us standing there and Nolan on the floor.

"Holy hell, he's drunk as a skunk," Nathan said.

Nash glanced at me.

"Hey! Don't look at me. Charlie called me."

Nolan sat on the floor, drunk off his ass.

"Okay, we need to get him upstairs and sober him up. It's a good thing that Ma and Dad are out of town for the weekend." Nash lifted Nolan off the floor.

"Hey, Nash. You're such a wonderful brother." Nolan raked his fingers over Nash's face.

"Yeah, yeah. Come on, drunky. Let's take care of you." Nash started up the stairs with Nolan. Then the front door opened.

We stopped dead in our tracks.

"How would I know the hotel was a flea-bit motel?" Nate asked.

"Read the reviews!" Pat said.

"Ma and Dad are home," Nixon mouthed.

"No, shit," Nash said. "Change of plans. Grab his other arm, Nix."

Nixon helped Nash as they came down the stairs.

That's when it happened. "Uh, I don't feel good."

Our eyes widened as Nash said in a whisper, "Get the door!"

Noah ran to the door, whipping it open. Nixon and Nash carried Nolan out. He puked everywhere, including on Nash, Nixon, and himself.

"That's gross," Nathan said.

Nash and Nixon shot him a glare.

"Boys! Where are you?" Pat asked.

"Shit! Ma's coming!" Noah said.

"Girls distract Ma. Nathan and Noah clean up the puke while Nix and I try to get him upstairs," Nash said.

Nash and Nixon carried Nolan around the house. Kat and I closed the door while Noah and Nathan cleaned up the puke.

"This is so gross," Nathan said.

Pat came downstairs. "Did you see the boys, Maggie?"

"Ah, nope. Kat is staying the night," I said.

"I am?"

I elbowed her.

"Yes, that is right. I'm staying the night."

Pat gave her a strange look and shook her head. "Okay."

"So, why are you home early?" I asked.

"Nathaniel booked us at this run-down motel. Something darted across the floor. I said that was it."

Nathan and Noah peeked over the windowsill, looking through the kitchen window. We stared at them.

She asked, "Do you hear water running?" She turned around, but they ducked.

"Um, no. There's no water running," I said.

"That is so strange. I thought I did. What's that smell?" Pat moved to the door. Nathan and Noah hid around the house's side. Kat and I stepped in front of her.

"It's a skunk," I said.

"Yep, you know how stinky those things are," Kat said.

"I'll check the garbage cans. When boys left the lids off the last time, a wild animal tore open the bags." She reached for the door handle, but we stopped her.

"We'll check for you," I said.

Kat nodded in agreement.

"Oh, nonsense." She turned the handle. The twins darted around the corner. They ran towards the front of the house to Nash, Nixon, and Nolan. Pat secured the lids and came in. "That is so odd."

"What is?"

"I don't remember that it rained," she said, looking at the wet cement.

"Michigan weather can never decide," Kat said.

It's true. Our weather was beyond bipolar. You never knew what you were getting weather-wise.

"Nope." I shook my head while agreeing with Kat.

"Well, I'm going to bed. Tell the boys we'll see them in the morning."

Nash came through the front door as I waved my hand by my hip. He left, closing the door. Pat turned, and I hid my hands behind my back.

"Night, girls," she said.

"Night, Pat," we said.

The kitchen door opened with the boys coming through it. "We need to get him upstairs before someone else appears," Nash said, trying to hold onto Nolan.

They started up the back steps when the light flicked on. Nate sat on the top step. "Is there something you would care to tell us?"

We sighed. So much for trying not to get caught.

"Uh, I don't feel good," Nolan said.

"Outside now!" Nash said.

He and Nixon carried Nolan out. Nolan heaved, emptying his stomach's contents.

Nate walked outside. "Nash and Nixon go upstairs and clean up. I'll take care of drunky over here. The rest of you go to your rooms. We'll discuss your punishments tomorrow. Come on, party boy. It's time to hose you off." He turned the hose on Nolan and sobered him up quickly.

"Dad!"

Nate whistled while spraying Nolan. When he finished, Nolan looked at him while shaking. "You want to drink and have fun? You'll have fun staring at your four walls for the next two weeks."

Nolan walked by.

"Oh, and Nolan?"

He turned and looked at his dad. "You and I will talk about the pleasures of underage drinking tomorrow."

Kat and I sat on my bed when my door opened, and Nash and Nixon walked in.

"How's Nolan?" I asked.

"Sober. Dad hosed him off outside." Nash chuckled.

"I still can't believe he did that. We told him no," Nixon said.

"Well, he's young and dumb," Nash said.

"What do you think our punishment is?" I asked them.

"We tried to hide his drunken state. They'll ground us," Nash said.

"Aren't you too old for grounding?" Kat asked him.

"I'm a Gray. I'm never too old for grounding," he said.

They sat on the floor while we sat on the bed, talking, when Nate said, "Nash and Nixon! I said your rooms, not Maggie's room!"

"Here we go," Nixon said.

They got up. Nixon kissed Kat, and Nash gave me one. It'll be his last kiss for a while.

"So, you and Nixon kissed and made up."

"Yeah, we talked. Then, well, we stopped talking." A smirk formed on her lips.

"Ew."

"The first time it happened, Nixon was nervous. That's why it was so awkward. After that, the boy showed his moves." She giggled.

I hugged my pillow.

"Maggie? What's wrong?"

"I'll disappoint Nash when it happens between us. I'm a virgin, and he has experience." That idea made me insecure.

"Have you talked to him about it?"

"I'm afraid to talk to Nash. Nash is twenty soon to be twenty-one, and I'm a high school kid." I sighed.

"Nash isn't as shallow as you assume he is with sex. Yeah, he has experience. I learned from Nixon that these boys don't take sex for granted. They're not one-night stand guys."

"Maybe."

"There's no question about it. Girl, have you seen the way he looks at you? That boy is head over heels in love with you."

"What? I assumed he liked me a lot."

"Oh, no. Nash might not say it, but that boy is crazy about you. Trust me."

Huh? Is it possible? I'll find out whether he is or not.

CHAPTER 23

18 AND I 🤍 YOU

Maggie

After Nolan's drunken escapade, I didn't get to talk to Nash. Nate and Pat had confined us to our rooms for a week. Nolan got a lecture, along with a two-week grounding for his stunt. He's lucky.

We endured solitary confinement in our rooms. Pat and Nate planned my eighteenth birthday. I had to hand it to them. They did enjoy their cake. Any reason to have cake, they did. They threw me a birthday party.

I pondered what Kat said. Was Nash in love with me? Is it possible?

The party was in full swing, and everyone had a splendid time. I like my freedom. It sucks to get stuck in a room on purpose. Nothing says I care about you like getting grounded.

We enjoyed the party. The best part was the gifts. The boys chipped in and gave me a new phone, my friends gave me jewelry, and Nate and Pat gave me clothes. They're typical Mom and Dad gifts. Then came Nash's contribution.

"Happy birthday, Mags." He handed me a small box while sitting next to me on the couch.

"Thanks, Nash." I took the box from him and opened it. Everyone smiled as I pulled off a lid to show a heart-shaped necklace. I held it in my hand. "It's beautiful. Thank you."

"There's more."

He was right. There was a folded piece of paper. I opened it, and it read: *I heart you.*

"I heart you, too," I said. Yep, I'm oblivious to things.

"Um, Mags, it means I love you."

My head turned toward him. "What?"

He got down on his knees and gazed at me. He took the necklace from my hands and held it. "I had the necklace engraved and wanted you to know my feelings."

I took the necklace from him and turned it over. Engraved in tiny words, I love you. "Then shout it to the world." Yeah, I like a good challenge.

He leaned into me. "I love you."

"Why did you whisper it to me?" Our faces are mere inches from each other.

"Because you are my world."

I smiled and blushed. I leaned towards Nash. "I love you, too." With that, he kissed me.

"Well, it's about damn time!" Nixon said.

"Language!" Pat said.

"Sorry, Ma."

We laughed. Leave it to the Grays to ruin a moment.

A loud banging sound came from outside as we had cake and ice cream. Nate opened the front door. "You gotta be kidding me!"

Pat walked over to him. "Now?"

Why are they yelling? I walked over to them, getting one hell of a surprise. I walked outside as someone pounded on a signpost in my front yard. Then they hung a for sale sign on it.

Great. Not only did my parents dump me, but they put my childhood home up for sale on my birthday. Yep, my parents were outstanding.

"Maggie," Nate said.

I turned around and faced everyone. "Yep, it's official. My parents hate me and leave it to them to ruin my birthday." I walked back inside and ran upstairs.

"Why would they do that?" Noah asked them.

"They're self-centered tools. They don't deserve Maggie," Nate spoke through gritted teeth.

"That poor girl. My heart aches for her," Pat said. "I'll check on her."

Nash stopped her. "Let me." She nodded as he headed upstairs. He walked to my door and knocked, but I didn't answer. He opened the door to see me sitting on my bed. "Mags?"

I sighed as Nash sat next to me. "Why do my parents hate me so much? Am I that bad?"

"No, they're self-centered assholes. They don't see what a great woman their daughter is. When we were kids, I used to think you were the biggest pain in the ass."

"Is this supposed to make me feel better? It doesn't."

"You didn't let me finish." He chuckled. "As we grew up, I noticed how much you had changed. Instead of trying to hang out with us, you did your own thing, and I missed you."

"Is that why you gave me a challenging time?"

"Yes. I was hoping to get your attention. You hadn't shown us attention anymore as you outgrew us, which bothered me. When you turned fifteen, I noticed you more, and my pants tightened more."

I gave him a weird look.

"But I was dating Sarah. So, finding your fifteen-year-old neighbor girl beautiful was unnerving. When Sarah and I broke up, I figured I would ask you out. Then I found out that you liked that tool. Well, I figured it wouldn't happen. So, I backpacked through Europe for a year. I figure the crush I had on the neighbor girl would go away."

"Wait. You had a crush on me? On me?" Okay, his news shocked me.

"Yep, now let me finish."

"Okay. Sorry, you may continue."

"Well, I came home to find a girl sleeping in my bed. Being dark, I didn't realize who it was, but I needed to thank Ma and Dad later. I remember the scent of coconuts from your hair. I like that smell. When I found you in my bed the next morning, I realized I needed to thank Ma and Dad."

I laughed.

"I didn't think you would feel the same way about me. You liked Bryson and had these hopes. It burned me to hear you say his name. Who was I to crush someone's dream?"

I never knew Nash felt this way. I always assumed he hated me, along with his brothers.

"Well, if we're confessing, I have one."

"Oh, yeah? Go on."

"When I was younger, I had a crush on you. Well, you and Nixon, but don't tell Nixon."

"Nope."

"If I bothered you guys enough, you would pay attention to me. As I grew up and figured that would never happen, I moved on. I realized you guys were mean, so I figured it's best to move on. I moved on to liking someone that I shouldn't have. Hindsight is twenty/twenty, I guess. I found I liked you more when we learned about each other."

A smile curled upon his lips. "So, I guess confessing my love to you is for the best?"

"I would say so."

He tapped his finger to his lips. "Hmm."

"What?"

"Oh, nothing." He shrugged.

"Nash, what is it?"

"I thought about how good that sounds."

"What?"

"I love you, Mags. It has a nice roll off the tongue."

"Hmm, let me try. I love you, Nash. Yep, you're right. It has a nice roll off the tongue."

He leaned over and kissed me as we heard a collective "aww." We turned to see everyone standing there.

He got up, holding out his hand. I took it as we walked back downstairs.

"So, you had a crush on me?" Nixon asked me.

"Yeah, I'm not sure what I was thinking."

"Ouch, that hurts." Nixon placed his hand over his heart.

"I'm sure that you'll survive." I smirked.

Nash took my hand, leading me downstairs.

"Psh, women."

The brothers laughed.

My eighteenth birthday didn't turn out how I had planned. It ended how it should.

CHAPTER 24

THANKSGIVING WITH THE GRAYS

Maggie

It's an event when you spend a holiday with someone else's family besides your own. It's a unique adventure when you celebrate the holidays with the Grays. Eight people in one house made for a fascinating dynamic. You throw in added family members, making the holidays pure chaos.

Pat and Nate cooked dinner as the boys watched the Lions lose again. I'm not too fond of sports. I curled up in a chair, reading a book. They would yell each time the ref called or miscalled a play.

Ding Dong!

"Will someone answer the door?" Nate asked.

The brothers ignored the doorbell due to the football game. I didn't feel comfortable enough to answer it either. The person got impatient, lying on the doorbell.

"My family can't be bothered. Here, let me get it." Nate walked by and answered the door.

"Well, it's about damn time you answered the door, big brother."

"Jonas! What are you doing here?"

The boys stopped and walked over to find their Uncle Jonas at the door with two guys.

"Hey, Uncle Jonas." Nash hugged the guy.

"Hey, Nash, Nixon, double troubles, and little man," Jonas said. "Will you let us in, or should we freeze to death?" He smirked.

"Come in, Jonas. Where's Karen?"

"At her parents. She didn't want to make the trip. So, I brought Jace and Jamie with me. Go mingle with boys while I catch up with my big brother."

"Whatever," Jaime said.

Two guys walked in with the brothers. They looked similar in features. I'm guessing they're cousins since the guy named Jonas called Nate his big brother.

"Who's playing?" One guy asked Nash while glancing at the TV.

"The Lions and Packers." Nash took a seat on the couch.

"Packers suck ass. I hope we kick their asses." The guy rubbed his hands together.

"Who's the chick?" The other guy asked Nixon.

"That is Maggie. She lives with us and is Nash's girl, so don't even think about it, Jaime."

"I don't know what you mean."

"Sure, you don't. If you make a move on Maggie, Nash won't hesitate to put you into the ground."

"So, uh, did you ever try?"

"No."

"Well, damn. I would have hit it."

"Uh, Jaime. One more comment from your mouth about Mags, and I'll knock out your teeth." Nash glanced at Jaime while the other guy, I'm guessing was Jace, chuckled.

"Psh, whatever." He went into the kitchen.

"I was good with being an only child. My parents thought I needed a playmate," Jace said.

"Tell me about it." Nash rolled his eyes.

I went to get a drink. Jonas helped Nate and Pat with dinner while Jamie stood with his back against the counter. I didn't know the Gray family well. I knew the boys and Nate and Pat while growing up. Their cousins came over, but I had never met them.

I walked over to the cupboard. "Excuse me."

Jamie shifted so I could get a glass. "You're the neighbor girl who followed Nash and Nixon around like a puppy dog, aren't you?"

"Excuse me?"

"Did I stutter?"

"For your information, I didn't follow them around like a puppy dog. I lived next door. Nixon and I are around the same age."

"Only because my aunt and uncle made Nixon and Nash play with you."

"Jamie!" Jonas said.

"What? It's the truth!" He glimpsed me. "My cousins tolerate you. Nixon can't stand you. Nash pities you."

"Jamie, enough," Nate said. "Maggie lives with us, and you won't talk to her that way."

"Come on, Uncle Nate! She's not even family. She's a girl who wormed her way into this family."

"Excuse me. I lost my appetite." I left the kitchen and walked past the boys.

"Mags?"

I didn't bother to look at Nash or any of them. Jaime's comment confirmed what I felt for months. I headed to my room, locking the door.

Nash rushed upstairs and tried the door handle but found it locked, then knocked. "Mags?"

I didn't respond.

Pat and Nate came up afterward. "What's going on?" Nash asked them.

"Jamie took it upon himself to belittle Maggie," Pat said.

"Great." He sighed. "What did he say to Maggie?"

"Nixon hates her and that you pity her," Nate said.

"That asswipe has always been jealous of us," he said.

"Nash! Language! He might be an asswipe, but he's still family," Pat said.

"If she doesn't come out, we'll have a funeral," Nash said.

"What? Why?" Nate asked him.

"Because I'll kill Jaime."

Nate, Pat, and Nash tried to get me to come out. The rest were going rounds with Jamie, especially Nixon.

*****

Nixon

"Why would you say that?" I asked.

"It's the truth. Don't deny that you told me how much you couldn't stand the neighbor girl," Jamie said.

"Yeah, I can't stand her. I don't hate her. What boy likes girls hanging around when they're kids?"

"I do," Nolan said.

We glanced at Nolan.

"What? I do."

"You even said it yourself. Nash felt sorry for her," Jamie said.

"No, I didn't. I said Nash didn't want to be mean to Maggie. Do you make it a habit of taking what we say out of context?" I asked.

"Come on, man. She isn't even family."

"Jamie. No one says you have to be blood to be family," Jace said.

"It's not right."

"Why, because we like her?" Nathan asked him.

"Come on, Nathan. You know what I mean."

"No, we don't. Since you've gotten here, you've had a chip on your shoulder. Now Maggie locked herself in her room. Why? So, you can feel better about yourself."

"Whatever."

"Whatever is always your response. Man, grow up," Noah said.

"Where is he?" A voice boomed.

"Ah, you pissed Nash off. You better run, little brother," Jace told Jaime.

"I'm not afraid of big bad Nash."

"No, dude. You better run," Nathan said.

"What will he do?"

Before anyone answered, Nash's fist flew, and Jamie lay on the ground out cold.

"That," Nolan said.

"I told him that he should've run," Jace said.

*****

Maggie

I sat on my bed, staring at the wall, not wanting to talk to anyone. Someone tapped on my door. "Maggie. It's Kat, Hunny."

"Go away, Kat."

"Please, open the door and talk to me. I promise it's only me."

"Is it only you?"

"It's only me."

I answered the door. Kat waved behind her for someone to leave. She walked in, and I closed the door.

"Do you want to talk?"

"Did Nixon call you?"

"Nash did after Nixon told him to call me after punching out his cousin."

"What?" My eyes widened.

"Nash isn't happy with his cousin now. Come on. Let's talk." Kat guided me back to the bed. We talked for a while, and I explained what had happened. She gave me excellent advice. I love Kat because she knows how to help.

"Maggie," a voice said from behind the door.

"Yes?"

"You have a distraught boyfriend planning his cousin's funeral if you don't come out."

Okay, that wasn't Nate or the boys. Who the heck was it? I opened the door to Jonas.

"Hi." He waved and smiled at me.

"You're Nate's brother."

"The one and only. I'm the middle one and the fun one."

"Hey! I'm fun!" Nate said.

"In your dreams, old man!"

"I might be old, but I can still kick your ass, you red-headed stepchild!"

"Yeah, whatever!"

I giggled at Nate and Jonas. Yep, they're brothers.

"See! I got Maggie to smile! So, bite me, you tool!" Jonas looked down the hallway.

"Nah, I don't bite anything that ugly!"

"Excuse me while I beat my brother's ass." Jonas walked away.

Nate and Jonas bickered. Someone picked me up, tossing me over their shoulder.

"Nash!"

He walked to his room, shutting the door. He set me down, then kissed me. "Sorry, I wanted to kiss you."

I gazed at Nash.

"My cousin was wrong and jealous. I don't pity you. I love you."

I regarded him.

"Say something."

"Did you punch out your cousin?"

"Well, yeah."

I threw my arms around his neck and kissed him. "I love you, too."

"Good."

"There will be no funerals until after the holiday."

"Deal." He led me out of his room.

After that, dinner went better. Jamie nursed a black eye, and everyone got along. Nixon and I came to an understanding. Thanksgiving turned out to be a delightful family meal.

CHAPTER 25

BEING ALONE

Maggie

During Thanksgiving break, Nate and Pat took the four younger boys to Nate's brother's house. They left Nash and me alone, but it's not what you think. I wasn't ready to be "alone" with him.

We watched a movie and lay on the couch, snuggled under a blanket. Nash laid behind me as we were on our sides. As the film played, he gave me soft kisses on my neck. I turned to face him, and we kissed. He moved his hand until he undid my pants, then slid his hand inside my panties.

He found his way between my legs, hitting a specific spot as my breathing hitched. My body moved with his hand as we kissed. He inserted a finger inside me. I let out a small moan against his lips. He applied slight pressure with his thumb as he continued.

As my body moved, so did his hand until I grasped his shirt. I let out a groan as my body twitched against him. I closed my eyes and lay there, breathing hard, coming down from this weird high.

I opened my eyes. Nash wiggled his fingers at me while smiling.

"What was that?"

"That, my dear, Mags, was your first orgasm."

My eyes widened. "Are you serious?"

"Yep."

"Whoa."

He kissed me. "Don't worry. I know you're not ready for the next step."

"It doesn't bother you, does it?"

"No. Why?"

"Most guys are in a rush. My friends have done it."

"Well, everyone goes at their own pace."

"So, does it hurt?"

"A girl's first-time hurts. Sex is tough when we first breakthrough. Most girls aren't used to us, and they're tight."

I sat up.

"What?"

I furrowed my brows. I didn't know how to talk to Nash about sex. I had so many questions.

"Mags, what do you want to know?"

"How did you know?"

"Because I can read your face. Ask me anything."

I thought for a minute. "How many women have you been with?"

He held up his hand and wiggled his fingers.

"Five?"

"Uh, huh."

"When did you have your first time?"

"I was fourteen. I messed around with this girl, and it happened. It didn't thrill her dad since the girl was thirteen. During my sophomore year, I dated the next girl, the third girl being Sarah. I had met the last two girls in Europe. European girls are way different from American girls, but it wasn't for me."

I sighed.

"What?"

"I'm afraid I'll disappoint you."

He pulled my chin to face him. "Hey, look at me. When it happens, it's because we love each other. Sex is an intimate, private act shared between two people. It is for me. Trust me. I don't discuss sex with anyone, not even my brothers."

That made me feel better. I didn't need Nash's brothers to find out.

"Anything else?"

"Can I see it?"

"See what?"

I pointed at his lap.

"You want to see my member?"

"Well, yeah."

"Okay." He pulled the blanket down and undid his pants, pulling his manhood out of his pants. My eyes got gigantic. Holy hell, it was big. Not only big but long and thick. He put it away and buttoned his pants.

"Satisfied?"

"Um, yeah." My face was on fire. Oh, dear God. Nash would put it inside of me. Let's hope I'm comatose when sex happens.

The rest of the night, we watched movies. After Nash's brief show and tell, he could tell I wasn't comfortable doing anything else. In time, but tonight was not the night.

$$\star\star\star\star\star$$

The next day, four obnoxious brothers awoke us.

"And what were you two doing last night, hm?" Nathan asked us.

"Sleeping," Nash said while rubbing his eyes.

"Yeah, sure, you were," Noah said.

"Was someone playing doctor? Did you ask Nash to bend over and cough?" Nixon smirked.

"No, we weren't playing doctor. No, I didn't ask him to bend over and cough." I rolled my eyes.

"How was Uncle Cayson's?" Nash asked.

"Rough. I swear the triplets get worse each year," Nixon said.

"Nix's mad because the devil spawn sprayed canned cheese over his face while he slept." Noah grinned.

"I swear, I'll beat their asses one day," Nixon said.

"The triplets?" I asked.

Nash propped himself. "Uncle Jonas has Jace, who is my age, and Jamie, who is Nixon's age. Uncle Cayson is our dad's baby brother. He has a set of triplet boys named Carson, Cody, and Caleb. They're the same age as the twins. The triplets are crazier than the demon spawn."

"How crazy?"

"Don't get caught alone with the devil spawn."

From the sound of it, the triplets were nuts. I would meet them soon enough.

"Where's Ma and Dad?" Nash asked his brothers.

"They're in the kitchen. Ma and Dad figure we would give you enough shit for them." Nixon smirked.

"Well, tell our parents not to worry. We did nothing that would cause Mags to get knocked up."

I wanted to hide under the covers. I don't know whether I should worry or not.

We walked into the kitchen.

"Is Maggie still intact?" Nate asked.

I glimpsed Nash as the others snickered.

"Yes, Dad. Maggie is still intact." He rolled his eyes.

"Just checking." Nate made a cup of coffee.

Nash leaned down. "I'll get a hotel room when it happens."

I didn't turn pink, but a tomato.

"I'm so glad that we don't visit your brother often," Pat said.

"Cayson isn't that bad."

"No, but his boys are something else." She made a cup of coffee.

"What happened?" I asked. "From everything I'm hearing, it sounds like they're the devil spawn themselves."

Everyone laughed.

"Something like that," Nate said.

"Carson, Cody, and Caleb sprayed Nixon's face with canned cheese. They took the twin's clothes, leaving them naked. We won't go there with Nolan." Pat recounted their stay at Cayson's house.

"Yes, please don't." Nolan shifted in his spot. I don't want to learn what they did to poor Nolan. It had something to do with his underwear.

Yep, I'm not sure I wanted to meet the triplets, aka the devil spawn of Cayson Gray.

CHAPTER 26

WEDDING INVITES

Maggie

Okay, before you think crazy, I'm not getting married. I turned eighteen. Nash and I weren't to that point. Plus, I'm still in high school.

We received an invitation to Sarah and Mike's wedding. In case you forgot, Sarah was Nash's ex, who is marrying Bryson's big brother. The wedding should be exciting.

*****

Pat

"Do we have to go?" Nathan asked.

"Yes," I said.

"Why?" Noah asked.

"Because I RSVP for us."

"Whom the hell goes to your ex-girlfriend's wedding? It's abnormal," Nixon said.

"Hey, if your mom is forcing me to go, you're going," Nate told the boys.

I gave Nate an annoyed face.

"What? I hate weddings," Nate said.

"I still talk to Sarah's mom. Plus, it wasn't on bad terms."

"Sarah hooked up with Nash's best friend while they were together and is marrying a tool. Mike is a bigger tool than Bryson himself," Nixon said.

"Tool or no tool, if your brother doesn't have a problem with it, neither should you."

"Only because Nash doesn't know," Nathan said.

"What do you mean Nash doesn't know?"

The brothers looked around, whistling.

"Nixon Richard Gray! What doesn't Nash know?"

"Sarah cheated on him with Mike," Nixon said.

"How do you know?"

"Yeah, I'm curious, myself," Nate said.

"Nathaniel!"

"What? I'm always out of the loop. Plus, I like to gossip next to the next person."

I rolled my eyes at Nate and turned my attention back to Nixon. "I'm waiting."

"Fine. We caught Mike and Sarah together," Nixon said.

Nate and I stared at him and the others.

"Coming out of a hotel. Trust me. They weren't visiting someone."

"What were you four doing at a hotel?" Nate asked Nixon.

"That's not important," he said, avoiding the question.

Nate glanced at me. "I don't want to know why our boys were at a hotel. Do you?"

"Oh, God, no."

*****

Maggie

The six of them were downstairs discussing the wedding. Nash and I were upstairs talking about nothing. We were busy doing other things.

"Oh, my God, Nash! Keep going!" I gripped the sheets of his bed as he had his arms wrapped around my legs while he had his head between my legs. He blared his music so no one could hear us.

He went to town. I couldn't control myself as pleasure ripped through my body.

*****

Nate

"Why the hell is Nash blaring music?" I looked at the ceiling. The boys tried not to laugh.

"He needs to turn that music down. I swear he'll wake the dead," Pat said.

I thought for a moment. "Where is Maggie?"

"Beats me." Nixon shrugged.

Pat and I glimpsed each other. We ran upstairs while the boys roared with laughter. We reached Nash's door, and I pounded on it. "Nash! Open up!"

Nash opened the door. "What?"

We stuck our heads inside to see Maggie lying on her stomach, looking at a magazine. She turned her head and looked at us.

"Why's your music so loud?" I asked him.

"I wanted to get a feel of this new album I bought. I'll turn it down." Nash walked over to his stereo and turned it down.

"Well, next time, try not to play it so loud."

"No problem." Nash shrugged.

We left.

*****

Maggie

Nash crawled into bed next to me.

"That was close." I sighed.

"Well, I wouldn't have to crank my music so loud if you weren't loud." He smirked.

I smacked him.

"You're loud. Note to self. Make sure I buy you a gag." He chuckled.

I gave him a playful shove. We wrestled until he pinned me by sitting on top of me.

"Do you want to attend this wedding?"

"Yeah. Why?"

"I have concerns about the wedding."

"It'll be fine. The wedding is a month away. It gives us plenty of time to find an outfit."

"Easy for you to say. You guys get to throw on a suit and call it good. Girls have to find a dress, shoes, accessories, makeup, and any other crap that we need."

"Mags, even if you dress in a burlap sack, you're beautiful to me." He smiled at me. "Plus, it's a wedding. We'll go, eat, and dance. Then we'll come home and move on with our lives."

I had a terrible feeling about this wedding. It wasn't that Bryson and Tiffany would be there. Something else will happen. I'm overthinking things.

*****

The house became hectic with school, the wedding, Christmas, and New Year's. Why does this time of the year get crazy?

People lose their minds over one day. In our case, it was two days driving everyone crazy. During the chaos, I found out when Nash's birthday was. A person turning twenty-one is a big deal.

Pat and Nate would plan a party for him. I wanted to do something special.

Around midnight on Nash's birthday, I was the first to wish him a happy birthday. I pulled a single cupcake from a package and placed a candle on top. Then I opened my door.

Everyone was asleep until I saw Nash's light underneath the door. Perfect. He was still up. I knocked and opened his door.

He glanced up from his book. "Mags? I figured you would be asleep."

I crept in. "Well, I wanted to be the first one to wish you a happy birthday. So, happy birthday." I pulled the cupcake from behind my back and lit the candle.

He sat up and took the cupcake from me.

"The cupcake isn't much. It's the thought that counts, right? Make a wish."

"I don't need to make a wish."

"Why not?"

"Because I have you."

I smiled.

He blew out the candle. "Sleep with me."

I gave him a weird expression.

"I want to cuddle with you. Sleep with me."

"As long as you don't knock me up." I pointed my finger at him.

He rolled his eyes, pulling me to him. We climbed into bed, covering ourselves. I snuggled into him and drifted off to sleep.

Nate checked on us and saw me in bed with Nash.

Pat walked up. "What's taking you so long?"

"That." He pointed to us, sleeping next to each other. "I give up. He's twenty-one. If he knocks her up, then it's on him."

Pat laughed while Nash and I slept.

CHAPTER 27

CHRISTMAS FUN WITH THE GRAYS AND THEN SOME

Maggie

Christmas arrived, and our senior year was flying by. Nash and I were closer than ever, including the rest of the Gray family. Life with the Grays became second nature, except it took a little time for me to become a family member. I bickered like a sibling, and I became excellent.

"Nah, nah, nah, you can't catch me." Nolan gave me a raspberry.

I chased him for stealing another bra. "Want to bet?"

"I bet you five bucks she catches him," Nixon told Nash.

They stood in Nash's doorway, watching us.

"I'll take that bet," Nash said.

"What's going on?" Nathan asked.

"Maggie will give little brother a beating for taking her bra," Nixon said.

"I have five on Maggie," Nathan said.

I tackled Nolan, punched him in the stomach, and yanked my bra out of his hand.

"That was harsh," Nolan said.

"Well, you deserved it." I got up. "Stay away from my bras, you perv!" I marched to my room with said bra in hand.

"Did she need to punch me?" Nolan asked his brothers from the floor.

They said, "Yes."

"Boys! Can you come down here and bring Maggie?" Nate asked.

"Go on. I'll get Mags," Nash told his brothers.

They came downstairs, and Nash got me. When he opened my door, he got hit with a pillow.

"If we have a pillow fight, I prefer you naked in my bed."

I gave Nash a skeptical expression.

"It was a suggestion. Come on. The rents want us."

I walked out of my room with Nash. We walked downstairs to the living room.

"Now that you're here. We have a surprise for you," Nate said.

"Is it another car?" Nixon asked him.

"No."

"Is it a new TV?" Nathan asked him.

"No. And where is your better half?"

"He's at Marcy's house, getting lucky."

Nathan shrugged. Nate shook his head.

"Are we getting out of that stupid wedding?" Nixon asked.

Nate gave him a peer. "No, and you're still going."

"Well, there goes that idea," he said.

"We're getting company."

"Who?" Nash asked.

Before Nate answered, someone, knocked. Nate walked over and answered the front door. We heard a male's voice.

"Oh, no," Nathan said.

"Are you serious?" Nixon asked Pat.

She shrugged. "Your dad thought it would be nice to have the family for Christmas."

"What does your mom mean?" I asked Nash.

He didn't have time to answer.

"Who do we have here?" Someone asked.

We turned to see three guys standing in front of us.

"Maggie, say hello to Carson, Cody, and Caleb. Uncle Cayson's kids and the devil spawn themselves."

My eyes widened as my mouth became agape. Oh, boy.

The triples faced us with devilish smirks while Cayson and his wife, Dominique, came in with Nate and Pat.

"Who are you?" Carson asked me.

"This is Maggie," Nixon said.

"Did I ask you? No, I asked her."

Okay, I was not too fond of Carson.

"Maggie, who?" Asked Cody.

"Our next-door neighbor, Maggie," Nathan said.

"They're deaf, dumb, and stupid," Cody told Carson.

"Yep," Carson said.

I was not fond of Cody either.

"Wait a minute! Aren't you the girl who followed Nash and Nixon around like a puppy dog? I notice you made it out of your awkward phase with braces and pimples. No offense, but you were ugly," Caleb told me.

I stared at him, stunned. Yep, it's official. I was not too fond of the triplets one bit.

Nash put his hands on his hips. "I get that you're the devil spawn, but one more word out of your mouth, and I'll knock you the hell out."

"Yeah, we'd like to see you try, big man," Cody said.

Nash shrugged. "Okay. You asked for it."

Pat and Nate walked into the living room with Cayson and Dominique. It was a sight to see. Nash, Nixon, and Nathan had the triplets pinned to the floor.

"The boys are getting reacquainted." Cayson smirked.

"A little help here, Pops," Carson said.

"Nope. You three have big ass mouths. I'm surprised Nate's boys are going this easy on you."

Their visit would be fun.

*****

Nate and Pat rearranged everyone's sleeping arrangements. Cayson and Dominique had Nash's bedroom, while two triplets had Nixon's bedroom. Nash had to bunk with Nixon. The twins ended up bunking together while Carson and Cody shared a room. Nolan got stuck with Caleb. I got lucky and had my bedroom.

For a seven-bedroom house, the family visit cramped us. Then issues started.

"Hey, Noah. God called. He wants his Ark back!" Cody said.

"Screw you, Cody!"

"Hey, Nixon. Weren't you impeached years ago?" Carson asked.

Laughter followed.

"Piss off, Carson!"

"Knock it off!" Nash said.

"Someone's mad because his tv show got canceled." Caleb snickered.

"I swear to God. I'll beat your asses if you don't knock it off!" Nash said.

"Yeah, I'd like to see you try, big man!" Carson said.

"Nolan, what's with the magazine? Oh, never mind. We have a magazine here, and everyone gets a turn," Caleb said.

I refuse to let the triplet twits degrade me. I whipped open my door and stormed over to Nolan's bedroom. I knocked, and everyone opened their door.

"Yes?" Caleb asked me.

I balled my fist, cocked my arm, and let it rip. I punched Caleb in the nose, causing blood to spew from it.

There was a collective "ooh" from everyone.

Caleb grabbed his nose. "You broke my nose!"

"Good, you vile, little rat!" I turned to Carson and Cody. "You two shut the hell up! No one cares what you think. If we want your opinion, then we'll give it to you. Until then, keep your damn mouth shut." I stormed back to my room and slammed the door.

"I'm in love." Carson sighed.

"Yep," Cody said.

"You're too late, you knuckleheads. She's mine," Nash said.

"Maggie will fit in with this family," Cayson told Dominique.

"Yep," Dominique said.

Caleb nursed a broken nose the following day while Nash and I decorated the Christmas tree. Carson and Cody had plans of their own. I went upstairs to get more decorations from the storage closet. I closed the door to find Cody standing there.

"Hey, Maggie."

"Hi, Cody."

"Did you need help?"

"Nah, I'm good."

"Here, let me help you." He took the decorations from me. That was weird.

I came downstairs and walked over to Nash.

"Where are the decorations?" Nash asked.

"Cody has them."

"Why?"

"I'm not sure. Cody had a creepy tone to his voice."

Then Carson waved at me with a smile.

"Sort of like Carson right now." I pointed at Carson.

Nash turned to notice him giving me the eye. He turned back to me. "Yeah, I would stick close to me if I was you."

"Why?"

"When my cousins take an interest in someone, they take an interest."

"Should I feel creeped out or flattered?" I smirked.

Nash glanced at me.

"Kidding. I'm kidding."

"You better be kidding." He wrapped his arm around my waist and pulled me close to him. "Because you belong to me, baby girl."

Holy hell, that's hot when he called me baby girl and said that I belonged to him. My inner self was doing a merry dance. Who'd thought the neighbor boy would be with me? I didn't.

Carson and Cody tried to sit by me at dinner, but Nash and Nixon edged them out. Nash did it because of being overprotective of me. Nixon did it to piss them off for the cheese incident. Caleb glared at me. Oh, well. He shouldn't have made his comment about me.

"So, Maggie. I haven't seen you since you were little. How are you?" Cayson asked me.

Without missing a beat, I said, "Besides my parents dumping me on the Grays, putting my home up for sale on my birthday, and dealing with crazy Gray family members. I'm okay."

Everyone stopped. What? It was the truth.

"Well, you're handling it well," Dominique said.

"Yeah, sure. If it weren't for Nate and Pat, I would be homeless." I didn't mean to sound sarcastic, but their questions bugged me. They were trying to be nice but asking about my shitty ass parents irked me.

"So, Cayson, how about the Lions?" Nate asked.

"Man, do we need to talk about how crappy our home team is doing?" He contorted his face.

Nate gave me a quick wink. Thanks for the save, Nate.

After dinner, we opened gifts. Then Carson and Cody caught me under the mistletoe. Fantastic.

"So, it's tradition to kiss under the mistletoe." Carson wiggled his eyebrows at me.

"Yeah, pucker up, baby." Cody puckered his lips.

"That's a dumb tradition, and we aren't celebrating it." Nash grabbed the mistletoe and walked to the door. He opened the door and chucked the mistletoe outside.

"Man, why do you have to ruin our fun?" Cody asked.

"Because I can. Now, excuse us." Nash led me into the kitchen.

"Thanks for the save." I sighed.

"What are wonderful boyfriends for with their girlfriends? Now, pucker up." He held the mistletoe over his head.

I snickered. "I thought you threw out the mistletoe."

"Optical illusion." He shrugged.

I pulled him into a kiss. Nash always made me feel better. That's why I fell for the neighbor boy.

CHAPTER 28

ALL HELL BREAKS LOOSE AT A WEDDING

Maggie

Since Sarah's parents had invited the Grays to the wedding, the girls attended with the boys except for Nolan. He didn't have a date. The girls were getting ready in my bedroom.

"Girls, hurry, or we'll be late!" Nate said.

"Beauty takes time!" Pat said.

"Can you, oh, I don't know, speed up the beauty process?"

"Oh, fine, but don't blame me if I have one false eyelash!"

We finished and came downstairs. I walked over to Nash

"You look beautiful."

"Well, you look handsome."

"Yeah, yeah. You're pretty. Nash is cute. Can we go, please?" Nate tried to usher us out of the door, taking three cars.

We arrived at the wedding on time and took our seats. I didn't understand why it worried Nate about us being late. The wedding ceremony was boring but nice.

The fun started at the reception or when all hell broke loose.

We found our assigned seats and sat down. Then the staff served us dinner. The food was okay. It was nothing I would brag about to people. If I ever get married, I want excellent food.

After dinner, the dancing started. It's your typical dance order at a wedding. Husband and wife first, then daddy-daughter, blah,

blah, blah. Afterward, Nate and the boys showed off their dance moves.

"What's going on?" I asked Pat.

"Watch, sweetie."

Nate walked over to the DJ and requested a song.

"Attention, everyone. A few people requested a song for a dance. Please, clear the dance floor," the DJ said.

Nate and the boys strolled out onto the dance floor. The DJ started the song, and so did Nate and the brothers. They danced in sequence while I stared in shock. They performed unified moves and were fantastic. People clapped as the guys moved together.

"Where did they learn to dance?" I asked Pat.

"Nate thought the boys should learn to dance. He said it was essential when they met a girl."

They finished, and everyone clapped. Everyone returned to dancing, and Nash walked over to me.

"That was amazing," I said.

"Yeah, we like to impress people with our dance moves." Nash smirked. "Do you want to dance?"

"I thought you would never ask." I smiled.

Nash led me onto the dance floor, and we danced. We had so much fun. Well, until an argument broke out between Bryson and Nixon.

"What now?" Nash asked.

We stopped dancing and walked over to them, yelling at each other.

"You're such a tool!" Nixon said.

"What's going on?" Nash asked Nixon.

"It's Bryson being Bryson."

"Your brother is mad because my brother won," Bryson said.

"Won what?" Nash asked Bryson.

"Sarah."

"It's not a competition," Nash said. "Sarah and I broke up a long time ago."

"If you say so." Bryson shrugged with a smirk.

"What does that mean?"

"Nothing, Nash. Let's leave this tool," Nixon said.

"No! I want to know what he means!" Nash turned to Bryson. "What did you mean?"

"You couldn't keep Sarah satisfied as much as my brother could." He smirked.

"What?"

"Damn, you're dumb. My brother had always planned to steal Sarah from you, and he succeeded. Guess the best man won. The Grays aren't all that."

Yep, the shit hit the fan.

Nash hauled off and decked Bryson. As Nixon and Nate tried to separate Nash and Bryson, the wedding got interesting. Mike and Sarah rushed over as the fight intensified.

"Is it true?" Nash asked Mike and Sarah.

"What's true?" Mike asked.

"Were you sneaking behind my back?"

"What? No!"

"Oh?" Nash glared at them with balled-up fists.

"Nash," Sarah said, confirming Nash's question.

He hauled off and hit Mike, causing Mike to crash into the cake.

"My cake!" Sarah said.

"Screw your cake. You're a cheating whore!" Nash said.

She glared at Nash. "I'm glad that we broke up! I don't regret cheating on you! Mike is ten times the man that you'll never be! I knew you had a thing for the neighbor girl. You always stared at her. You're a perv."

Oh, hell, no! I refuse to let her make nasty remarks about Nash. I smacked Sarah across the face.

"Damn!" The brothers said.

"Don't you ever speak that way about Nash! He's more of a man than your husband will ever be!"

"You're nothing but a worthless bitch!"

I lunged at her. We fell into the cake while wrestling. I wanted to rip out her fake hair extensions.

"Get off me!"

We struggled. I got in a few good whacks, and Sarah did too. Then they pulled us apart. Our hair was a mess with cake on our clothes and face.

"Nathaniel, you and your ungrateful brats need to leave," Sarah's father said.

Nate faced him. "Bob, I didn't like you in high school. I didn't like it when our kids dated. I didn't want to come to this abomination that you call a wedding. So, on that note, good luck with the divorce."

We left with Nate and Pat.

"Don't worry about sending us a Christmas card next year!" Pat said.

This evening was a mess. So much for a joyous occasion. Nash got hurt, and I was a big freaking mess. I must admit that it was nice when Nash hit Bryson and his brother. They both deserved it.

✼✼✼✼✼

I took a shower, cleaning the cake out of my hair and cracks. I put on clean clothes and found Nash lying on my bed while staring at the ceiling.

I sat down next to him. "Are you okay?"

He sighed. "Yeah. I should be angrier than I am, but I'm not."

"How come? Not that I didn't enjoy seeing you get ticked off, but I figure that you would be more upset than you are."

He propped himself. "But I'm not. Yeah, Sarah and I were together. She noticed how I looked at you. Many people knew it, except for me."

"What do you mean?"

He sat up. "When we were younger, I always saw you as my little sister. The pesky sister who wouldn't leave you alone."

"Um, thanks?"

"Come on. I was a kid. You went through your awkward phase. Then one day, you weren't this awkward, pesky little sister anymore. Do you remember when we used to talk at night?"

I smiled at the memory. "Yeah, I was in my bedroom reading, and you saw my light. You asked me what I was doing, and I told you. You started talking to me about books morphing into music and movies. You would always stop by and chat. I had a friend to talk to while growing up. Then, out of the blue, you stopped. I figured you hated me so that I would hate you."

"But I didn't hate you. I liked you. But you were only fifteen, and I was afraid it would cause problems for you. Sarah and I used to fight about it."

Listening to Nash made me remember those nights. I had missed them. Nash and I had become friends because of those nights.

"But Mags, I realized that I had feelings for you. I didn't know how to handle them. How can you be angry when you don't care about that person but someone else? Do you understand what I'm saying?"

"I can understand your point. You never have to worry about me cheating on you." I grinned.

He rolled his eyes, pulling me into a kiss. "You kicked ass tonight."

"I did, didn't I?"

He chuckled.

Mike and Sarah won't ever invite us to their house, and that's fine.

CHAPTER 29

RUN FOR COVER!

Maggie

I awoke feeling like a bus had hit me as a pain shot through my pelvic area. Fantastic. It's when Mother Nature decides to rip your uterus into two. You have bloating and crankiness while consuming an insane amount of chocolate.

I not only struggled with that time of the month, but Pat did too. Two women on their periods made for an exciting time in the Gray household.

Pat and I watched a program on TV while sitting on the couch and cried.

"But it's so sad," I said.

"I know."

Nate walked in, confused. Why the hell were we crying? We must be watching a dramatic movie. He saw the Snuggle commercial as he glanced at us. "Christ." He walked over to the bottom of the stairs. "Boys!"

The brothers came downstairs.

"Yeah, Dad?" Noah asked.

"Your mother and Maggie have started."

The brothers glanced at our weeping asses.

"What do we do?" Nathan asked.

"We go to the store, buy them chocolate, then throw the candy at them and run."

Nate wasn't negotiating. The brothers did what their father told them to do. We were weeping messes on the couch.

*****

Nate

The boys and I headed to the store, strutting to the candy aisle with the chocolate. We tossed chocolate bars into the shopping cart, ensuring we had plenty.

"Should we get Ma and Maggie a card?" Noah asked.

"Who gets a girl a card while on their period?" Nixon asked.

"I don't know. Sorry that your uterus hates you or something." Nathan shrugged.

Nash walked away.

"Now, where is your brother going?" I asked.

"Nash is searching for a period card," Nolan said.

*****

Nash

I stood in the tampon section.

"If you buy Maggie a product, then buy this brand." Kat held out a box of tampons.

I took them from her. "Thanks. I don't buy feminine products."

"No worries. Most guys don't. Where's Nix?"

"He's with my dad and brothers buying chocolate and lots of it."

"That bad?"

"Two women on their period at the same time at my house? What do you think?"

She laughed.

Kat and I walked over to the cart. I tossed the box into the basket.

Kat kissed Nixon, glancing at the cart. "Well, you boys have your bases covered."

"Considering Pat and Maggie are a weeping mess on the couch, I would say so," Dad said.

"Take this bottle to them." Kat tossed them a bottle of Midol to Dad. "That should help."

"And that's why I love you," Nixon said.

"It helps when you're the one with the uterus in the relationship." She giggled.

"I'll skip going home," Nixon told Kat as they left together.

"Coward!" I spoke.

Nixon waved.

"Let's get home before your mother and Maggie turn into raging hormonal messes," Dad said.

We left the store, returning with the candy. We tossed us Midol, tampons, and lots of chocolate while Ma and Mags sat on the couch. We left the room.

*****

Maggie

Pat and I shrugged and tore into the candy. When I wasn't a raging hormonal mess, I would need to ask Nash about their shopping trip.

Later, I took a hot bath to relieve my cramps. I climbed into the tub, closed the shower curtain, and lay there. The door opened and closed.

"Mags?"

"Nash?"

"Oh, thank God." He took a seat on the floor next to the tub and leaned back against the wall.

I peeked out from behind the shower curtain at him. "Dare I ask why you're in here?"

Items crashed. "Run for cover, boys!" Nate said.

"That's why I'm here."

"What in the world?"

"Nolan made the mistake of taking a chocolate bar in front of Ma."

"Is your brother dumb? You never take chocolate from a woman while they're on period."

"Young and dumb."

I laughed, then stopped and sat forward in the tub. "I've been thinking."

"About?" He cocked an eyebrow.

"About me being ready to have sex."

He became silent.

"You said you would wait, but I'm ready."

He gazed at me. "Are you sure? Because you only get one first time." He tried to gauge my reaction.

"I know. I want my first time with you."

He leaned toward me. "Okay, but I want our time together to be romantic. Every girl deserves a romantic first time."

"The question is when."

"It should happen when it happens. Maggie, if you're not ready, we can wait."

"Oh, thank God because I'm not ready."

"I knew it! You said that to test me, didn't you?"

I shrugged.

"For that, you'll get it."

"What are you doing? Nash!"

Nash climbed into the tub while clothed and tickled me. I squealed with laughter as he sat back and faced me. I brought my knees to my chest to cover myself.

"Don't worry, baby girl. When sex happens, I'll take excellent care of you."

My cheeks heated. Damn, Nash was hot when he called me baby girl.

The bathroom door opened. Nate stared at us in the tub. "I don't want to know." He closed the door behind him.

We laughed. Heaven knows what the Gray family will assume when we had sex. We could wait because sex wasn't everything to us. There was so much more to us. When sex happened, it would be worth the wait.

CHAPTER 30

MY DARLING VALENTINE

Maggie

Valentine's Day is when couples spend a romantic day with dinner, movies, and gifts. I'm celebrating my first Valentine's Day with someone. I wasn't sure what to expect. With the Grays, you never know what to expect.

We didn't expect Nixon to get arrested. Yeah, I'm still trying to wrap my head around that scenario which involves Nixon, Nolan, and a hooker. I should rewind so we can get a clear-cut picture of what happened.

*****

Nash had planned a particular date for us. He made reservations a few weeks ago at a romantic restaurant that included dancing. While we were getting ready for our date, Nixon decided to help Nolan with a slight issue. Well, Nixon didn't help him but got dragged into the matter.

*****

Nixon

My phone rang. "Hello?"

Nix? Are you at home?

"Nolan? Yeah, I'm getting ready to leave. Why?"

I need your help, and don't tell Ma and Dad.

"This phone call can't be good. Where are you?"

Nolan gave me the address, and I hung up. As I was leaving, Nash stopped me.

"Where are you going

"Nolan asked me to pick him up at an address."

"Nix, our reservations are for seven."

"I know. Do me a favor and pick up Kat. I'll meet you guys there."

"Okay, fine, but make it quick."

I left to pick up Nolan, then returned to my double date with Nash, Maggie, and Kat.

*****

Maggie

Nash knocked on my door as I was getting ready.

"Baby girl, you look stunning."

"Well, thank you, sir. I'm almost ready."

"We have to pick up Kat along the way."

"Why?"

"Got me. Nixon said he had to get Nolan. He said that he would meet us at the restaurant." He pulled me to him and kissed me.

I wiped the lipstick from his lips, and we left to get Kat.

*****

Nixon

I pulled up to an address, got out of the car, walked to the door, and knocked. A lingerie-clad woman answered it.

"Well, hello, sugar. What can I do for you?" She smirked.

I glanced at the address, assuming I had made a mistake. No, the address was correct.

"I'm looking for a young, tall, dumb, and horny kid."

"That kid? He's with Laci. I can do whatever you want."

"Uh, no thanks. I'm here for the kid."

"Follow me, sugar." The woman led me to a room.

Women lounged around dressed in lingerie. What the hell did Nolan do?

"Laci! Someone is here for the kid!" The woman said at the door.

"Hang on! We're almost finished!"

I opened the door and got a view of Nolan with the girl.

"Nixon!"

"Nolan, get dressed!"

"Nixon? Like the disgraced president?" The woman asked me.

I glared at her. "Do you have a problem with my name?"

"Nope."

Nolan got dressed and made his way to the door.

Then someone said, "Hell! It's the police!"

"Shit. It's a raid!" The woman pushed past us.

Our eyes widened as we ran, only to get caught by the police.

"Hold it right there! Hands up!" The police officers pointed guns at Nolan and me.

We raised our hands. The police took our hands, moving them behind our backs and

"Don't worry about Ma and Dad killing you. I'll kill you myself when we get out of here," I told Nolan.

The police led us to the police car.

*****

Maggie

We sat in the restaurant waiting on Nixon.

Nash got impatient while Kat and I sat there, hungry. "I'm sorry about my idiot brother."

"Yeah, I'm sorry too." She gave him an awkward smile.

I felt terrible for Kat. The evening should have been lovely.

Nash's phone rang with an unknown number. He answered it after the third ring. "Hello?"

Nash?

"Yes."

Man, you must help us!

"Nix?"

Nash's response got our attention. We leaned forward as Nash talked on the phone. "Where are you?" He listened as Nixon explained. Then he asked, "Jail? Why the hell are you in jail?"

Kat and I glimpsed at each other and mouthed, "Jail?"

"Uh, huh. Uh, huh. Yeah, we'll be there. Oh, and Nix, tell Nolan that I'll kill him." He hung up. "Sorry, ladies, but we must leave."

We left the restaurant and endured a silent car ride. Kat and I glanced at each other, then shrugged. Nash fumed. When your brother calls you from jail, you have two questions. One is why, and two is why. It's the same question, but you can't help but ask twice.

We pulled up to the police station and entered through the front entrance. Nash walked to the front desk and spoke with an officer.

"How much trouble are Nixon and Nolan in?" Kat asked me.

"A lot."

We waited while the officer took Nash to the holding cells.

*****

Nash

Nixon and Nolan were standing in a jail cell.

"Oh, thank God, Nash," Nolan said.

"Nolan, what the hell were you thinking?"

Nolan gave me a sheepish expression.

I cut him off before he answered. "Never mind. You weren't thinking with the right head." He glanced at Nixon.

"I thought Nolan was getting into trouble at a buddy's house. I showed up at a hooker's house. He called because he was short on cash," Nix said.

We glared at Nolan.

"Man, the police think that I'm a pimp. I tried to explain that I was on my way to dinner with my girlfriend."

"Well, I have both girls here and explained everything to the officer."

"What did you tell the cops?"

"The truth about you meeting us and having to pick up our little brother. Our little brother is a complete idiot."

"Sounds about right." Nix smirked.

"Nolan and Nixon Gray! You're free to go." An officer unlocked the cell.

My brothers stepped out of the holding cell.

"You're lucky. Next time, you won't be. Stay away from those places," the officer told Nolan.

"Y-yes, sir."

We walked to the front.

"Now what?" Nix asked me.

"Well, we drop the little weasel off at home and still have our date. The date will be a little unusual."

*****

Maggie

After we dropped off Nolan, Nash drove us to a diner. No, Bryson didn't work there. We didn't want to ruin the rest of our night with the slightest chance of seeing him.

"How will you explain tonight to your parents?" I asked while eating my burger.

Nash and Nixon glanced at each other.

Nash said, "We aren't. He is."

"Ma and Dad won't let him see the light of day," Nixon said.

"What was Nolan thinking?" Kat asked.

"Well, he thought he didn't want to be a virgin."

"And how did that go?" I asked Nixon.

"Not well. When I found Nolan, he had almost finished. We'll need another cake." Nixon smirked.

We laughed. Ah, blue balls, the gift that keeps on giving.

After we ate, we went dancing. It was so much fun. Nash and Nixon tore up the dance floor with their moves.

Nash pulled me into his arms and danced with me. "I'm sorry about my brother ruining our night."

"I wouldn't say that he ruined our night but altered it. Plus, I didn't need a fancy restaurant when I can't pronounce the dish's name." I giggled.

"I wanted to impress you." Nash sighed.

"Nash, you don't have to take me to fancy restaurants or buy expensive items to impress me. Trust me. I grew up having money. Someone who loves and cares about you is better. Snuggling on the couch while watching a movie is more important to me."

"I didn't need to do this special date." He arched an eyebrow at me.

"Well, I like the dancing part, but I'm good if we keep it low-key." I smiled.

He looked into my eyes. "That's why I fell in love with you, Mags. You enjoy the simple moments."

"Good. It hurts to love someone on Valentine's Day, and they don't love you back. I spent four years pining for someone."

"Well, not anymore, baby girl. If I have my way, you'll never spend another Valentine's Day alone ever again."

"I love the sound of that idea."

"And I love you." He leaned in and kissed me.

We had a few minor bumps, but tonight turned out perfect. I wouldn't have it any other way.

CHAPTER 31

SNOW DAYS

Maggie

I should catch everyone up with what happened since Valentine's Day. Nash and I kept our romance simple and made our relationship much better. Nixon and Kat were going strong, as were the twins with Marcy and Macey. As for Nolan, he tried to hide what he did until his brothers ratted him out. Not only did Nolan get a blue cake, but his brothers razzed him. He couldn't leave his room for a long time.

Nate and Pat weren't happy with what he did, getting himself and Nixon arrested. He's lucky that his parents took it easy on him.

Everyone hung at the Gray's house for the evening when the snow started. I love Michigan weather because it can't make up its mind. Mother Nature needs to change her meds. Since it's still February, it's not only freezing but snowing.

It begs the question of whether we have a snow day. It would help if you had exceptional circumstances when you lived in a northern state to get a snow day. Most schools stay open unless you live far north or live out in the boonies, aka the countryside. The rest of us get to suffer, trudging through this arctic wasteland that we like to call Michigan. Come on. It shapes our state as a mitten which is ironic.

We played Monopoly since the weather confined us indoors. Someone was always a sore loser at this game which was Nixon.

"This game blows." He got up and went into the kitchen.

"I take it that Nixon hates to lose," I said.

"Lose? Nixon hates any game that he can't win." Nash chuckled.

"Every game," Nathan said.

"It can't be that bad," Kat said.

"Oh, it's bad. One time, Nixon played Candy Land with Nolan. He lost and threw the board game out of the door," Noah said.

"That's bad," Marcy said.

"Yep," they said.

"So, what happened to Nolan?" Macey asked us.

"Nolan needs to think with his head on his shoulders and not with the one between his legs." Nash rolled the dice.

"We thought Ma and Dad would kill him when they found out," Nathan said.

"Did your brother tell your parents?" Kat asked them.

"Nope, we ratted out his little ass," Noah said. "Although, the cake was delicious."

"Cake?" Marcy asked.

"Don't ask." I shook my head.

We continued playing with Nixon rejoining us. Hanging out was fun. We talked and laughed when Pat's phone rang with a recorded message.

She came into the living room. "You don't have to go to bed early tonight. They canceled school for tomorrow."

Everyone cheered. No one was leaving because of the snowstorm. Then the power went out.

"Nate!" Pat said.

"I'm checking, Pat!" Nate came up from the basement. "It's not the breaker box. It has to be from outside."

We stood.

"Grab the wood from the garage, Nash, and Nixon. Get Nolan and gather blankets and pillows, Nathan and Noah," Pat said.

Nate gathered candles and flashlights. He brought in a percolator and coffee so that we could have a warm drink. Nash and Nixon brought in wood to make a fire. After getting a fire started, Nate made coffee over the fire.

Nathan and Noah returned with Nolan and lots of pillows and blankets. If we get stuck here, we'll make the best of it.

The girls snuggled with their guys under the blankets. Nolan snuggled next to Pat while she sat next to Nate.

"So, Pat, you told me about you and Nate, but you never told me the entire story," I said.

"Oh, you don't want to hear about us." She tried to brush it off.

"Sure, we do," Marcy said.

"We don't even know the full story. So, spill, Ma and Dad," Nash said.

"Go ahead and tell them," Nate told Pat.

She sighed. "Well, Nate and I were neighbors. His family lived across the street from my family, and my older brother was friends with them. You had Nate, Jonas, and Cayson. I was the little sister they never had and fair game for them to tease."

"We did it out of fun. Patricia took it to heart. She would get so mad at us. It's what siblings do, right?" Nate asked us.

We nodded.

"But I had a huge crush on Nate. I was always afraid to tell him. Plus, with the teasing, we didn't get along."

"Until one day, I saw a boy pick on her. No one could pick on her except for us."

"Thanks a lot."

"Well, it's true. It wasn't until I saw what the boy had done to Patty. She didn't deserve it, and I took matters into my own hands."

"Nate's actions surprised me. After that, we started talking more. The night of my birthday, he gave me my first kiss and asked me out."

"How old were you?" I asked her.

"It was my eighteenth birthday."

"Yeah, she wasn't jailbait." Nate chuckled.

She smacked him and rolled her eyes. "When we had our first date, Nate's mom handed him a compact package. She told him not to forget his raincoat because she didn't need grandbabies."

"My ma embarrassed me in front of Patty."

Pat laughed.

"After that night, if she could handle my crazy mother, I would marry her."

"But I didn't know if I wanted to marry him. We dated and danced around the idea. Then seven months later, we got married. Eighteen months later, Nash arrived, followed by Nixon.

Two years later, Nathan and Noah arrive, then Nolan. I never thought I would marry the boy across the street."

"Well, my ma knew."

"Heck, yeah, she did. She kept talking about us when I was fifteen." She giggled.

I laid on Nash while listening to Nate and Pat. I loved hearing their story. It was so romantic. Two people who grew up together had ended up together. They gave me hope. Nash rubbed my arms with his hands and kissed the top of my head.

Listening to Pat and Nate talk about their courtship made me realize how I felt about Nash. I snuggled into him.

We talked and laughed. Everyone fell asleep except for Nash and me.

"You've been quiet," he said.

"I've been thinking."

"About?"

"About us."

"And?"

"I'm ready."

"You're messing with me again, aren't you?"

"No, I'm ready."

"You're serious."

"Like a heart attack."

"Okay. I want to do it right. I'll get a hotel room and make it romantic. I want it to be special for you."

"Okay." I pulled him into a kiss.

He kissed me back. Without a doubt, I'm ready to take the next step with Nash. It would be an unforgettable night for us. The question was when.

CHAPTER 32

SOLD

Maggie

After our snow day, life returned to normal. Nash and I will have our moment, but I had to worry about other things. I had the pleasure of coming home to the Gray's house and saw a sold sign on top of the for-sale sign.

I frowned. My parents had sold my home with the belongings which I wanted. I entered the house, heading straight to my room.

*****

Nixon

I got out of the car, followed by my brothers.

"Man, as much as we fight, that's shitty," Nathan said.

"I agree. Maggie doesn't deserve this," I said.

We walked inside as Ma met us.

"What's wrong with Maggie?"

"Is Nash home?" I asked her.

"No, he's helping your father at the plant. Why?"

"Look." Nathan pointed to the door.

She walked over and opened the front door. "Sonofabitch!"

"Ma!" The brothers said.

"Oh, please, none of you can act offended. You boys cuss worse than I ever did." She rolled her eyes. "I'll talk to Maggie." She turned and walked upstairs.

*****

Maggie

Someone knocked on my door. "Maggie? It's Pat, Hun. Can I come in?"

"No offense, Pat, but I'm not in the mood to talk."

"Okay, but if you change your mind, come find me." As she left, I sniffled.

*****

Nixon

We met Ma at the bottom of the stairs.

"How is Maggie?" I asked.

"Well, she's upset. I didn't think Maggie's house would have sold so quickly. The housing market hasn't been good."

"Are you calling Dad?" Noah asked.

"No, your father and brother will find out soon enough." She walked past us.

I pulled out his phone.

"What are you doing?" Nathan asked me.

"I'm calling Nash." I found Nash's contact info and hit send. "Nash? We have a problem."

Nash

Dad and I pulled into the driveway and saw the sold sign in front of Mags' house.

"Nix wasn't kidding," I said.

"We had better get inside. Maggie must be heartbroken."

We walked into the house. Dad found Ma as I went to see Mags.

I knocked on her door. "Mags, it's me. Can I come in?"

"Yeah."

I entered her room, closed the door behind me, then took a seat next to her. I wrapped my arms around her as she cried. "Shh, you're okay."

After crying for a few minutes, Mags sniffled. "It wouldn't be bad, but I want my stuff from the house."

"Is that why you're so upset?"

She peeked at me. "Well, yeah. I want my pictures and other items. Personal mementos that you can't replace."

I smiled. "I say that you should have your things."

"How?"

"I have an idea." I smiled.

*****

Maggie

Before anyone gets any bright ideas, no, we didn't break into the house. Nate called the realtor after Nash talked to him and persuaded her to let me go into the house to take whatever I wanted. After much cussing on Nate's behalf, she agreed to meet us at the place tomorrow after school.

*****

After school, the realtor met the boys and me at the house. She opened the door, shocking me. The people trashed the place. For the past few months, whoever rented my home did not take care of it.

"Damn. A bunch of pigs lived here!" Nixon said.

I had no words. I wanted to take what I wanted to keep. We climbed the stairs to my room. I opened the door to find my bedroom still intact. At least they didn't demolish my room.

We set the empty boxes down, and I packed my personal belongings.

"Aw, you still sleep with a teddy bear." Noah picked up my teddy bear off my bed.

I snatched the stuffed bear from his hands. "Don't touch, Mr. Fluffykins."

"Fluffykins?" Nash arched an eyebrow at me.

"Well, he's fluffy." I shrugged.

Nash shook his head and chuckled.

"Damn, Nash. Now I can see why you took an interest in Maggie." Nathan held up a pair of lacy panties.

He smacked Nathan on the back of his head. "Don't act like Nolan." Nash snatched the panties from Nathan's hands and then walked me. "Can you wear these one day?"

My cheeks warmed.

"Maggie, what's this?" Nixon pulled out a document.

"I'm not sure." I walked over and opened the document. I read through the papers, which looked like a legal documents.

Nash took the paper from me and read it. "The document looks like a trust. Who's Graham Holcomb?"

"He was my grandfather and my mother's dad. Why?"

"Because that's who signed the form." He pointed to the signature.

"That is weird. I didn't know my grandfather well because he died when I was six."

"Here's an envelope," Nixon said.

The envelope had no address on the front. I found a letter.

Dear Margaret,

I hope you're doing well. I am writing this letter to explain the secret document you had found. Why is an older man hiding stuff? I understand, my daughter. Money was more important to her than people. She found a man like your father, who's greedy.

You'll find a binding and legal trust with money that I have set aside for you in the document. Part of the trust will pay you when you turn eighteen. The rest comes when you turn twenty-five.

Margaret, I wanted you to have an excellent start in life. I tried to clarify things for you. Money doesn't make us rich. The people in our lives do. The ones who care when we have nothing and still love us are the riches you'll ever need in your life. Cherish them because, nowadays, they're a rare commodity.

Please don't tell your parents. I don't want them to take money from you, for it's not theirs to take.

Love

Papa

I stood in the middle of the room, shocked. I had a legal document under my nose and didn't realize it. The money was nice but meant little to me.

Nathan whistled. "That is many zeros."

"Can your dad look at the document?" I asked Nash

"Yeah, sure. Mags, if the trust is real, are you moving out?"

His brothers stopped and looked at me.

"I haven't thought that far ahead. If the trust is legit, I would prefer to go to school. Then I'll figure things out along the way," I said.

"You can always stay and attend a local college. That way, you'll have a home-cooked meal," Nixon said.

"And a comfy bed to sleep in," Nathan said.

"Along with brothers who would pester you." Noah shrugged.

Nash leaned down. "Plus, if you move, I won't get to see you before bed and after you wake up."

I glanced at the brothers who awaited my response. "I guess I can stay longer and finish school, then go to college."

"Oh, yeah, because education is essential," Nash said.

"Sure." I sighed. "First, let's pack my stuff, then we can go from there."

With that, they helped me pack. I took what I wanted and the pictures that meant the most to me.

My grandfather was right. Things don't matter, but people do. The Grays gave me a place when they could have said no. They didn't, which made me grateful. To me, they were family. So, why would I leave their family?

I had a perfect idea if the money was legit. My idea would mean something to everyone, including myself.

CHAPTER 33

THE PRODIGAL PARENTS RETURN

Maggie

Nate took the paperwork to an attorney friend. The paperwork had issues that we overlooked. Besides the money, there was the matter of the house. My parents sold other possessions, and part of the money was missing. Someone signed my name, dated the day of my birthday, on extra paperwork. It's illegal.

Gee, who could have that been?

The attorney sorted through my parents' mess. It left me in a holding pattern which was fine. It's not like I need the money now.

*****

Nate

Someone did a quick tapping on the door.

I opened it. "Brian! Tricia! What are you doing here?"

"We came for our daughter," Brian said.

I glared at him. "The one you dumped here and disowned? That daughter?"

"That is none of your business, Nathaniel."

"Brian, when I have a teen girl whose parents throw her away, it becomes a part of my business. But I'll get Maggie." I went up the stairs.

The boys met me in the hallway when I raised my hand and shook my head. I knocked on the door, and Maggie opened it. I explained what was happening. We walked downstairs with the boys following us.

*****

Maggie

"Margaret!" My mother walked toward me and hugged me.

My arms dangle by my side. First, I hated when people called me Margaret, and my parents knew it.

"It's so good to see you, my darling." She acted loving towards me.

Second, my parents were not loving. They were cold. Affection was foreign to them.

"We came back for you."

They both faked a smile. Okay, this was the final straw. My parents never smiled and were never happy to see me. I was a thorn in their side. It was for show, and they knew it. Well, I did, too.

"That is nice."

"Aren't you happy to see us?" My father asked.

"The prodigal parents have returned! Isn't that fantastic?" I made a significant gesture with my arms.

The Grays tried not to laugh.

"That isn't a respectful way to act towards us, Margaret," my father spoke.

He tried to act authoritatively toward me.

"You have stayed with the Grays for far too long," my mother said.

I gave them both an unimpressed expression. "It's who I am. You would know that if you bother to give a shit about me! Oh, that's right! You dumped me on people who didn't want me here." The Grays protested, but I put my hand up. "But guess what? Can you guess? They decided, hey, this girl wasn't too bad and would rather have me stay than leave." I turned to the Grays. "Am I right?"

"Oh, yeah," the Grays said.

"Just checking," I said, then turned back to my parents. "Why are you here?"

"We told you. We came back for you," my father said.

"Bullshit! You not only dumped me but told Nate that you're done with me. You put my home up for sale on my birthday and never called once to check on me. So, I'll ask again and be honest." I crossed my arms and furrowed my brows.

My outburst shocked them, but I didn't care. My parents didn't deserve my respect.

"Well, we need you to sign papers," my mother said.

"What papers?"

"These." She reached into her bag and pulled out documents.

I snatched them from her and looked through them. "You're not serious."

"What is it?" Nate asked.

I shoved the papers at him.

He flipped through them, scanning them. "These are legal documents requesting Maggie to give you access to her trust," he said.

"What? Let me look at those." Nash took the papers from Nate as the others looked at them.

"The only reason you want access to my trust is that you're broke. Let me guess. You blew your money."

They fidgeted in their spot.

"Unbelievable!" I steamed.

Nate fumed and let loose on my parents. Boy, did he ever. I stepped back by the boys as Nate went off on them. He used every cuss word out there and more.

"Is that even possible?" Nathan asked Nixon.

"I don't even think that's legal," Nixon said.

"How many cuss words are there?" I asked Nash.

"More than I recognized."

"Who realized Dad had such colorful language?" Nolan smirked.

Nate almost threw an object at my parents during his tirade.

"Furthermore..." He added more colorful language to the mix.

When someone becomes furious, a tiny vein pops out of their forehead. Well, I'm sure Nate's vein would burst with his yelling. He stopped after a while.

"Well, I never!" My parents said.

"Yeah, and you never will again! Now get out of my damn house!"

They left as he slammed the door. He turned to me. "Maggie, you're an official member of this family. Those two people are the biggest tools I have ever met. For crying out loud, they are complete morons!" He walked into the kitchen.

"Sorry that your parents are tools," Nixon said.

I didn't know whether to laugh or thank him.

"What will you do with these papers?" Nash handed the papers back to me.

"Does anyone want to roast marshmallows?"

They smiled.

*****

We made a fire with the papers and roasted marshmallows. I didn't even care about the money. My parents thought they could waltz into my life because of money. It wasn't comforting.

My parents were the most significant tools on the face of the planet. I was lucky enough to be born to them. FML.

As we roasted marshmallows, Nash said, "Do you want to leave this weekend? We'll get away from everything."

I thought about it. "I like that idea."

"Good, I have a place in mind." He smiled at me.

I wondered what he was thinking. I mean to be alone with Nash all weekend. One thing came to mind. Oh, boy. This weekend will be one that I'll never forget.

CHAPTER 34

MISHAPS AND OTHER ISSUES

Maggie

Nash picked me up from school on Friday with our bags in the trunk. We made sure his brothers didn't realize what we were doing. We would have company if we did. Yes, they were that crazy.

I climbed into the car.

Nixon walked over. "Why are you here?"

"I'm taking Maggie out."

"Where?"

"Somewhere. Why?"

"I'm asking. Do Ma and Dad know?"

"Yes, little brother, they do. If you'll excuse me, we have somewhere to be." Nash rolled up his window and pulled out of the school parking lot.

*****

Nixon

"Was that Nash?" Nathan asked me.

"Yep."

"With Maggie?" Noah asked.

"Yep."

"Will we crash their date?" Nathan asked.

"What do you think?" I strolled to the car as my brothers followed.

"It'll be fun," Nathan told Noah.

"Yep," Noah said.

*****

Maggie

Nash drove until we pulled into a bed-and-breakfast parking lot. We got out, grabbed our bags from the trunk, then checked in, heading to our room. Once inside, we set our stuff down. The room had candles and rose petals and was perfect.

Nash walked over to me. "Are you sure?"

"Yes."

He placed his hands on my cheeks and gave me a soft kiss.

My heart raced as I tried to calm my nerves. "Why don't we undress and get into bed?"

Nash smirked. I stripped down to my underwear, and he did the same. I climbed into bed and pulled the covers over me. Nash followed suit. Man, my nerves were on edge. It was a big deal. There's no going back.

He hovered over me. "Are you sure?"

"Y-yes."

"Nervous?"

"Y-yes."

"Relax. I'll be gentle." Nash gave me a sly smile.

Oh, lord.

He hooked his thumbs into my panties and dragged them off me. I gulped. It's Nash. I have nothing to be nervous about with him. Then he wiggled out of his boxers and tossed them to the side. Scratch that, I became even more nervous.

He climbed off me, took a foil packet, and opened it. My eyes widened as he moved his hands under the covers. Oh, dear God, this was happening.

He rolled on top of me. "Baby girl, move your legs, or nothing will happen."

Nash calling me baby girl made my heart race. I moved my legs apart, and he positioned himself between them. Something touched me. I squirmed until he inched his way inside of me.

Oh, good God, this was happening. Something foreign was inside of me, which I'm not used to having inside of me. I let out a gasp while grasping Nash's arms.

"Relax. You're tense."

Hell yeah, I'm tense. Sex is nerve-racking. Nash adjusted himself as I gasped again. He slammed inside of me twice. Holy hell, sex hurts.

I groaned. Nash stopped until my body relaxed, then he kissed me. I kissed him back as he thrust in and out of me with a wave of pleasure flowing over my body. I rocked with him. He picked up the pace when I was ready, and my muscles tightened in my lower abdomen. We both groaned, exploding together.

I lay in bed with my eyes closed, enjoying this weird high. Nash chuckled.

I opened one eye. "What?"

"Looking at you in pure bliss from when we started. It's funny." He chuckled.

I smacked him. "Well, excuse me for being nervous. It was my first time."

"I know. Trust me. I know." Nash smirked.

"In my defense, you said it would hurt, but that was painful."

"I had to move fast the first few times to break it."

"Break what?"

He chuckled. "Your cherry."

I covered my face with my palms. Nash pulled my hands away and smiled at me.

"You're enjoying my embarrassment way too much."

"I can't help myself. You're cute when you blush." He kissed me.

Then someone knocked on the door. We both turned to look at the door.

"Open up!" A voice said.

We laid there.

"Open up before I break this damn door down!"

We looked at each other.

Someone busted open the door, and we jumped up. A guy stood there, looking mighty pissed.

"You slept with my wife!" The guy told Nash.

"Your wife? What do you mean? I'm here with my girlfriend!"

"That's not what my wife says! Now, I'll break you into two."

He lunged at Nash. Nash scrambled out of bed and fell onto the floor. I grabbed my panties, putting them on.

As the guy chased Nash around while Nash tried to cover himself, I heard snickering.

"Stop!" I spoke.

They both stopped as Nash covered himself with a pillow. I walked over, sticking my head out of the doorway. Nixon, Nathan, and Noah stood in the hallway and laughed. Nixon waved at me as I shot him a glare.

I walked back into the room and over to the guy. "His idiot brothers put you up to this, didn't they?"

"Well." He rubbed the back of his neck.

"How much did his brothers pay you?"

"Fifty dollars."

I nodded, then narrowed my eyes and lips. "Get out!"

"What?"

I pointed at the doorway. "Get out before I call the cops!"

"You don't have to tell me twice." He ran out of the room.

"Your brothers are idiots!"

Nash tossed a pillow aside and pulled on his boxers. He stuck his head out to see his brothers. "How did you find us?"

"Turn off find my phone feature, genius," Nixon said.

"Screw you, Nix. Now get out of here!"

"Nah, we'll stick around and hang out." He smirked. "Maggie, nice underwear." He gestured at my bra and panties.

I shot him a glare as they laughed. I walked back into the room.

"Poor baby, can't take a simple joke." Nathan snickered.

"Hello, Kat? Yeah, it's me. Is Marcy and Macey with you?"

"What's she doing?" Nixon asked Nash.

"She's calling your girlfriends." Nash smirked.

"What the hell?" Noah asked.

I walked out and held out my phone to them. "Your girlfriends would like a word with you."

Their faces dropped.

Nixon took the phone. "Hello? But baby. Yes. Yes. Yes. Okay, fine. We're leaving." He handed the phone back to me as they stormed out.

"I can't believe you called their girlfriends."

"It was that, or I call your mom." I shrugged.

"Girlfriends are a much better choice. Ma would say not to knock you up."

I laughed.

"Now, where were we?" He carried me back into the room and shut the door.

The next time was much better. I wasn't as nervous, and it didn't hurt. I laid on Nash as he wrapped his arm around me.

"I love you, Nash."

"I love you more." He kissed me.

I laid my head on his chest and drifted off to sleep.

*****

The whole weekend we didn't leave the room except to eat. It was nice to be alone with Nash. Sex was my new favorite activity. That weekend he showed me unique positions, and I won't walk for a while.

That boy has stamina.

We sat in a tub, taking a bath together. I leaned forward.

"What?"

"When was the last time you had sex?"

"About ten minutes ago." He smiled.

"Not with me. I meant another girl." I rolled my eyes.

"Let's see." He sat and thought for a minute. "A week before I came home from Europe."

"Was it a fling?"

"I'm not sure. I had considered staying longer because of the girl. She had gone back to her boyfriend. So, I came home." He sighed.

"I'm sorry." I touched his face.

"I'm glad it didn't work out. If it did, I wouldn't have fallen in love with you or had the chance to explore my feelings for you."

I beamed as he pulled me to him and kissed me, getting steamy.

It was a weekend that I would never forget.

CHAPTER 35

YOU'RE A TOOL

Maggie

After the weekend Nash and I had together, I couldn't stop thinking about it. My thoughts had gotten me all hot and bothered. I had to wonder if everyone had experienced their hormones raging. I needed a cold shower.

I started the shower and changed my mind about a cold shower after the water hit my skin. Yeah, a cold shower was a big fat no. I climbed into the tub as the water cascaded all over my body. The door opened and closed with the lock clicking. What the hell?

Someone let their clothes fall to the floor while opening the shower curtain and stepping inside the shower. I turned around and flinched. Nash stood in the tub in his full glory.

I smacked him. "You scare the crap out of me!"

Nash placed his hands on my waist, pulled me to him, and gave me a deep kiss. He grabbed my butt and squeezed as a soft moan escaped my lips. He trailed kisses to my ear. "We'll continue this later."

I arched a brow as Nash smirked, and I groaned. He was a tease.

We washed up, and he kissed me. We finished showering and dried off.

"I'll pick you up after school."

"Okay."

Nash pulled on his clothes as I got dressed. He kissed me and left the bathroom. I finished getting ready for school.

After breakfast, the brothers and I made our way to school. I got my books out of my locker.

"Oh, look, we have the girl with an undying love for someone she'll never get."

I glanced at Bryson and Tiffany. "You're such a tool." I shook my head while rolling my eyes and turned back to my locker.

"What did you say?"

"I said that you're a tool."

As I turned my head, Bryson's fist collided with my face. I fell to the ground while groaning.

"You should keep your mouth shut. Next time, I won't take it so easy on you." Bryson and Tiffany walked away.

I held my nose while groaning. I noticed blood and needed to get to the bathroom. When I tried to stand, I fell. The punch threw off my equilibrium. I crawled to my locker, trying to get to my phone.

Then someone said, "Jesus! Maggie!"

I saw two fuzzy people.

"Stay here. I'll get Nix," a shaky voice said.

The person must have been Nolan.

I grabbed my jacket and placed it on my face. Why won't the bleeding stop?

"Maggie!"

People rushed to me.

"Come on. You need help." The person helped me.

Another person said, "Call Nash."

✱✱✱✱✱

I sat in the emergency room while the doctor helped me. The doctor got the bleeding to stop and x-rayed my nose. Yep, Bryson broke my nose. My head throbbed as my eyes turned black.

"Sir! You can't go back there!" A nurse said.

"Like hell, I can't!"

I sat on the bed with the doctor standing next to it.

Nash walked up. "Jesus!"

"Here are two prescriptions. One is for pain. The other is an antibiotic. I want you to take them as soon as possible," the doctor said.

I nodded. The doctor left Nash and me alone.

"Oh, Mags."

"Can we go home now? My head is killing me."

"Yeah, come on." He helped me.

Nash brought me home and took me upstairs. I wanted to lie down. I walked to my room, but he guided me to his bedroom.

"Lie down on my bed. That way, I can watch you."

I didn't care what bed I was in at home. I wanted to sleep. Nash got me situated, and I closed my eyes. A broken nose was not fun and hurt like hell. You can't breathe. I wouldn't say I disliked Bryson, but I hated him.

✱✱✱✱✱

Nash

I came out of my room as my brothers walked up to me.

"How is she?" Nixon asked.

"In pain and tired. Can you get these prescriptions filled?" I handed Nixon the scripts.

"Yeah, sure." Nixon took the pieces of paper from me.

"What happened?" I asked Nixon.

"We don't know. Man, there was so much blood. Nolan found her because he was on his way to the bathroom."

I gave Nolan a look.

"To go pee," Nolan said.

"I want to know who hit Mags."

"What will you do?" Nathan asked me.

"I'll beat their ass."

"Sounds fair," Noah said.

My brothers left. I laid down with Mags.

*****

Maggie

I woke up, and my head throbbed.

"Easy. Here, take these." The person handed me two pills and a glass of water. I took them. The person took a seat next to me. "I would ask how you're feeling, but I can guess."

I glanced at Nash.

"Mags, who hit you?"

"Bryson."

"Why?"

"Because I called him a tool. Nash, I didn't see it coming. I turned, and his fist connected with my face. It happened so fast."

"Shh, it's okay." He tried to soothe me.

I leaned into his chest as he wrapped an arm around me. Tears fell down my cheeks.

"Lie down."

"You won't leave me, will you?"

"No, I'll stay with you." He laid next to me and pulled me to him.

I snuggled into him. At that moment, I felt safe.

*****

Nash

The following day, I went downstairs to get Mags some breakfast.

"How is she?" Ma asked.

"In pain." I seethed with anger.

"Who hit Maggie?" Dad asked him.

"Bryson sucker-punched her. Ma, can you prepare a plate of food for Mags?"

"Sure, Hun." She grabbed a plate, put food on it, then handed me the plate. "I'll call the school and tell them that she won't be in for the remainder of the week. Can you boys collect her homework?"

"Yeah, sure," Nixon said.

I left with a plate of food.

*****

Pat

"This animosity has gone too far," Nate told me.

"I agree."

"You and I should pay a visit to that school."

I nodded in agreement.

*****

Maggie

Nash brought up a plate of food and handed it to me. "Here, eat."

I didn't want to eat but didn't want to argue either.

"Ma called the school and told them what had happened. She said that you're staying home for the rest of the week. My brothers will collect your homework."

I protested.

But he put his hand up and stopped me. "It's Ma's orders."

One thing about the brothers, they never argued with their mother on essential matters. When they did, they found out that she was right. I was okay with it.

CHAPTER 36

PAYBACKS

Maggie

Pat and Nate told me they had spoken to the principal, who called Bryson into his office. Bryson denied any wrongdoing. Since they had no witnesses, it was my word against him. I'm a vengeful person trying to seek revenge on my crush. I swear the guy was a complete tool.

With his smarminess, he overlooked one detail: Tiffany. Where he goes, she goes. The brothers pay attention to details.

*****

Nixon

My brothers and I found Tiffany alone at her locker. I slammed her locker door shut, making her jump. "Hi, Tiffany."

"Hi, Nixon."

"We have a matter to discuss."

"What?"

"You were with Bryson when he hit Maggie," Nathan said.

"I don't know what you mean."

"That's a shame because Maggie told us," Noah said.

"What did she tell you?"

"That you and Bryson had ganged up on her. Fair is fair, right, boys?" I shrugged and nodded.

"What will you do?" Her voice trembled with fear.

I stepped back. "I'll slam your head into the lockers. Then go from there." I cracked my knuckles.

Her eyes widened. "You wouldn't."

"I would, and I will."

"But I'm a girl!"

"Do you think I care? Grays don't discriminate. We never have and never will."

We didn't care who you were or if you were male or female. We would dole out punishment to whoever crossed us. As a kid, I went after a neighborhood girl. She had gone after Nolan. I threatened to rip off her tits if she touched my brother.

"Fine. Yes," Tiffany said.

"Yes, what?"

"Yes, Bryson hit her!"

"It works for me. What about you guys?" I asked my brothers.

"Yep," they said.

"Now, we'll go to the principal's office. You'll tell him everything that happened between Bryson and Maggie," I said.

She huffed as we walked to the principal's office. Yeah, the situation wasn't great for Bryson and would get worse.

The principal called Bryson to the office after Tiffany recounted the entire event. The school suspended Bryson for two weeks and banned him from the annual senior trip. They cautioned him about retaliating against Maggie. They would not only expel him, but he would have to attend summer school to graduate. He's lucky to graduate.

The school should have expelled him.

*****

Nash

I waited until Mags was asleep to take care of what I had planned. I told my brothers that I was getting ice cream. Text me if Mags woke up. I wanted a plausible cover story.

While Mags slept, I drove over to Bryson's house with Nix. We got out of the car. I knocked on the front door only to have Mike answer it.

"What do you want?"

You could hear the contempt in Mike's tone. You couldn't blame him since I hit him at his wedding. However, Mike messed around with my girlfriend, now Mike's wife. The scenario had become so tangled.

"I want to see Bryson."

"Yeah, I don't think so."

"You can stay pissed at me, even though you were sneaking around with my girlfriend. What Bryson did was worse."

"What are you talking about, Nash? Bryson said a girl turned him in for cheating."

"You're kidding, right?" Nixon asked him.

"Nah, that's what he said."

"Damn, you're dumb." Nixon smirked, earning a glare from Mike. "Bryson didn't get suspended for cheating but for breaking Maggie's nose."

"Why would he break her nose?" Mike asked us.

"Because she called him a tool, and he sucker-punched her," I said.

"Oh, and he's the one who told Nash about you and Sarah." Nixon rubbed salt into the wounds.

Mike's face turned red. "Hang on. I'll be right back." He closed the door.

"That went well." Nixon smirked.

"You had to throw Bryson under the bus."

"Under the bus, the truck, the boat, it's all the same thing. Bryson is a tool and a liar. I'm helping him with finding the truth." He shrugged.

The door opened. As soon as I saw Bryson, I hauled and hit him square in the nose.

"Shit! You broke my nose!" He grabbed his nose as blood spewed from it.

"Eye for an Eye," I said. "Touch Mags again, and I'll break your hands and your legs." We started to leave when I stopped and walked toward him. "Why do you hate her so much?"

"What?"

"Maggie. Why do you hate her so much? You must have a reason since you crushed her at homecoming and tried to bully her on several occasions. Then you sucker-punched her. So, why?"

It's the one question no one had bothered asking until now.

"Because of what she said in her journal."

"That she liked you more than anything?"

"They said those things in front of my girlfriend." He pointed at Nixon.

"We did that to get back at Maggie, not embarrass you."

"Well, you did. You called me names and made me sound like a joke with a creepy stalker." Bryson groaned while holding his nose.

"We call everyone names, including each other!"

"Oh."

"Oh? That's all you have to say, oh? Unbelievable!"

"My bad."

"Your bad? You outed your brother at his wedding. You lied countless times and targeted a girl who liked you. All you can say is, my bad. You are a tool," I said with furrowed brows and shook his head at Bryson. "Come on, Nix. The longer I stay here, the more I'm prone to catching stupidity."

Nixon laughed as we strolled back to the car.

*****

Maggie

I awoke alone in a dark room, then got up and went downstairs. The Grays must be out somewhere since I didn't see them. My stomach growled, and I couldn't remember when I last ate.

I opened the fridge and scrounged for something to eat. I found lunch meat, lettuce, tomatoes, cheese, and mayo. I pulled it out and closed the refrigerator—a sandwich works for me. I'm hungry, but eating a big meal wasn't on the menu.

After making a sandwich, I sat at the table and ate. The front door opened, and I heard voices. They sounded like Nash and

Nixon's. I ate my sandwich as they did whatever. Then they yelled. Okay, no offense, but their screaming gave me a headache. It's not like my head wasn't already throbbing.

"She's in here!" Nixon said.

Nash ran downstairs into the kitchen. "What are you doing?"

"Eating. I was hungry." I gave him a slight smile.

He took a seat next to me. "How are you feeling?"

"My head is throbbing, but other than that, I'm okay." I shrugged.

"You look better."

I glanced at him. "I look like a truck hit me."

"Yeah, but you're still cute, baby girl."

His compliment would have turned me to mush, but my head hurt.

"I want to eat, then head to bed."

"Okay. You finish eating, and I'll lay down with you."

"So, how badly did you hit Bryson?"

"I don't know what you mean."

"Liar. I have a broken nose, not deaf."

He sighed. "I punched him once and broke his nose."

I gave him a glimpse.

"Hey, he deserved it."

"Oh, I don't doubt that. But why?"

"I didn't like what he did to you. Mags, he hurt you. He hurt you before, but this time was physical. I can't stand by and let someone I love and care about get hurt. It's not right."

I exhaled. "It's okay. I get it. Promise me that you're done with Bryson. I don't want to fight with Bryson anymore. I want to finish my senior year and graduate, then go to college."

"Fair enough."

I love Nash, but he needs to realize you can't beat up people. Yes, jerky people exist. You learn how to handle said jerky people.

CHAPTER 37

SENIOR CLASS TRIP

Maggie

For our senior class trip, we were going to Washington, DC. You would think we would be ecstatic about it, but we weren't. Why? Because this trip would be "educational," which means dull. Since my loving parents wanted to fight over my trust fund, I had no money to pay for said trip. FML.

I sat on my bed and worked on homework.

Nash strolled in. "Shouldn't you be packing for your senior trip?"

"Nope, because I'm not going."

"Why not?" He had his hands on his hips.

"Because Brian and Tricia had the courts freeze my trust until they decided. It meant no money." I went back to my homework. "No money means no senior class trip."

"Well, it's good that my parents paid for your portion."

My head snapped up. "What?"

"Yeah, they paid for yours and Nix's fee when they received the permission slips a few months ago."

"Why would they do that?"

"Because, as Dad said, you're a part of the family. Mags, when you know someone as long as we have known each other, you become family." He sat down next to me. "Plus, I'll be a chaperone."

"Huh?"

"They needed chaperones, and I signed up." He smirked.

"Uh-huh, sure. Is that because I'm going?"

"What do you mean? You said that you weren't going."

I gave him a playful push. "Shut up."

He chuckled, then leaned over and kissed me. I'm going on a senior class trip. Let's see. Nash was our chaperone. Nixon was going, and so were my friends. What could go wrong? Don't answer that question.

*****

I packed the previous night because I'm not a morning person. We had to arrive early at school. We stood with our bags and waited to get on the bus when I used Nash's back as a pillow.

"Look at Nash." Nixon chuckled.

"Someone needs to get Maggie a coffee, stat." Kat chuckled.

"Eh, she'll be fine. She's a little tired." Marcy shrugged.

"Listen up, Seniors. When we get to the hotel, we'll give your room assignments to you. Stick to your rooms. We have an itinerary for the trip. Stick to it. We don't need to call your parents and tell them that we lost their pride and joy," the teacher said. "Now, we need everyone to load their bags and board the buses."

"A little help here," Nash told Nixon.

"Come on, sleeping beauty." Nixon woke me and got me on the bus.

God, I need my bed.

I sat in a seat. Once we had settled into our seats, Nash took a seat next to me.

"Um, Mr. Gray? Since you're a chaperone, we prefer you to sit with the other chaperones and not a student," a teacher said

"He can sit with me," a woman said.

I woke up.

"I don't work for the school and volunteered to be a chaperone. I'm fine with sitting with my girlfriend." He shot a glance at the woman, who sat back down.

"Very well." The teacher sat down.

"I swear the teachers are as bad as when I attended school." I laughed.

The bus ride was long. When we arrived at the hotel, we had gotten our room assignments. I roomed with Kat while Nixon and Nash shared a room. Marcy and Macey shared a room. At least I was with someone I knew and liked. That was always a plus.

We settled in as I plopped on my bed.

"You never change." Kat giggled.

"I need to check to make sure the bed is comfy."

"Is the bed comfy?"

"Oh, yeah." I flailed around, making her laugh even more.

Someone knocked on the door.

"Come in!" Kat said.

Nash and Nixon entered and gave me a weird look.

"What? I'm testing out the bed," I said.

"It'd be better if I were testing it out with you," Nash said.

What was with him? He has been moody since the bus ride.

"Are you girls hungry?" Nixon asked.

"I'm starving," Kat said.

He held out his hand as she took it. I walked over to Nash as he walked away. Okay, whatever. It's his time of the month.

We talked at dinner. Nash responded to me with short answers, and his tone was off. So, I spoke to Nixon and Kat.

We returned to the hotel. Something was off between Nash and me. Will he act this way during the entire trip with him short with me, then ignoring me? Well, two can play that game.

*****

We got our itinerary and split into groups. The teacher who flirted with Nash was talking and laughing with him. Yet, he treats me like a second-class citizen.

When we returned, I headed to my room and left him to talk to her. I had worn out my welcome. As I lay on my bed while reading, Kat came in.

"There you are! We're getting something to eat."

"You go ahead. I'm not hungry."

"Are you sure?"

"Yep. I'll get something later."

"Okay." She shrugged.

*****

Nash

Kat came down to the hotel's lobby.

"Where's Mags?" I asked.

"She's still in our room."

"Why didn't she come downstairs?"

"Because you're a tool."

"How am I a tool?"

"Since we arrived, you have been short with her and offer no affection. You jumped the teacher yesterday."

"I didn't jump the teacher. I was being friendly. And for your info, I'm doing my job as a chaperone."

"By being a douche to your girlfriend? Excellent job, chaperone." She rolled her eyes and walked away.

"Fix this mess before tomorrow." Nix walked away.

I went to Mags' room and knocked on the door as she answered it.

I barged in. "What is your problem?"

"My problem? I'm sorry if my boyfriend is a king-size douche."

I furrowed my eyebrows. "That isn't fair."

"No, what isn't fair is how you're treating me. Since the bus ride, you've been acting like I'm nothing. Once we had engaged in sex, our relationship had changed. I'm not appealing to you anymore since you obtained the prize." Mags sat on the bed, frustrated.

"Is that what you think? That you don't appeal to me?"

"Yes. No. I don't know. It's not like I'm good at this."

I joined her on the bed. "Baby girl, you appeal to me more than you know."

She turned to face me. "What is wrong with you? You act like it's that time of the month." She raised her eyebrows and held out her hand at me.

I smirked and shook his head. "I figured if I were standoffish with you, we wouldn't want to tear off each other's clothes."

"That's the dumbest reason I have ever heard."

"It's a guy's logic. I want to strip you naked and ravish you right here."

Mags stood up. "Standoffish isn't so bad."

I chuckled and stood. "I'm sorry for being a doof. I want you right now."

"Lock the door."

I glanced at her as she gave me one back. Then I locked the door, and we had some alone time. It's good that Mags brought protection because I left my protection in my room.

*****

Maggie

I laid on Nash afterward, making circles on his chest with my fingertip. He had his arm wrapped around me as he stroked my arm with his free hand.

"Better?"

"Much." I propped myself. "Why were you flirting with the teacher?"

"I wasn't flirting. I was being friendly."

"You were flirting."

"Okay. Fine. I was flirting."

"You're a tool. Do you know that?"

"Yes, I know. Trust me. I know." He pulled me to him and kissed me before we continued another round. After that, we went again.

As for the rest of the class trip, Nash quit flirting. Well, after I flirted with another guy. You didn't think I would let him off the hook, did you?

The rest of the trip was fine. It was a little boring, but okay. Yes, we snuck into each other's room. You didn't think Nixon Gray wouldn't be alone with Kat, did you? It would never happen in a million years.

CHAPTER 38

MIDTERM HASSLES

Maggie

After our senior trip, we had midterms. How we did on our tests helped Nate and Pat decide if they let us travel somewhere for spring break or stay home. It was Nate and Pat's rule. To them, education was important. They've tried to persuade Nash to get more education under his belt, but he always made excuses.

I didn't understand his logic. Nash was brilliant and had potential, but he didn't want to apply himself and had settled. Nate and Pat had furthered their education. What stopped him?

I needed to find out and talk to the source themselves.

I knocked on his door and opened it. Nash was sitting at his desk while working on something. "Nash?"

He stopped and lifted his head, then turned to me. "Mags? Why aren't you studying?"

"I was, but I needed a break. What are you working on?" I walked over to him.

"It's something that I was working on." He tried to hide the paper.

I grabbed a piece of paper.

He tried to stop me. "Maggie, can you give that back to me?" He tried to take the paper from me.

I pushed his hands away and looked at the drawing. "Nash."

He rubbed his forehead. "I would have told you, but I figured it would have upset you." He tried to explain himself.

I studied the drawing. The definition was exquisite, and the details were flawless. Nash had captured my essence in the picture.

"The portrait is beautiful." I turned to Nash. "I didn't realize that you drew."

"I picked up sketching when I was a teen. I became bored. So, I picked up a pencil and started doodling."

"Nash, you have a real talent. Why aren't you pursuing art?"

"Because the idea is stupid."

"A gift is not stupid. Pursuing something you love is always worth it."

"If my dad and ma knew, they would tell me to grow up. I need to do something productive with my life."

"What do you mean?"

"That's another reason I had left. We fought about what I would do with my life. They wanted me to get a stupid office job that would offer stability. It's not me and never was." He sighed.

"Did you tell them about your artwork?"

"No, they wouldn't listen even if I did."

"Nash, I doubt your parents wouldn't listen. My parents, yes. Yours, no. It would help if you talked to them. Don't let a gift like yours vanish."

Nash had an eye for detail with a rare, raw talent. The drawing held proof. The ball was in Nash's court if he talked to his parents about art. He would waste his talent if he didn't pursue it.

*****

We studied for midterms. After becoming parched, I got something to drink and found Pat in the kitchen.

"Coffee?"

"Coffee sounds better than water."

"Are midterms getting you down?"

I sighed. "Yeah. Senior year is rough. Pat, can I ask you something?"

"Sure." She poured coffee into a cup and handed the cup to me.

"Did you know that Nash draws?"

"Yes. Why?"

"No reason." I left with a cup of coffee. If I discussed Nash, he would get upset. Nash was the guy who preferred not to talk about himself to others.

I had left Pat confused. I wanted to see if she knew if he drew or hid his talent from people. I hope he pursues art.

*****

Midterms came. Thank God. My brain had become so frazzled from studying. We got a break for two days after finishing them, which meant lots of sleep.

After I finished my last midterm and the others, we went home. We entered the house to overhear yelling.

"We told you that you needed to do something with your life!" Nate said.

"College isn't for me! I told you that!" Nash said.

"Nash, you're twenty-one! Figured it out!"

"I'm done talking about it!"

"Walk away! That's what you do well!"

Nash stormed past us and out of the door. The boys shook their heads and went upstairs. I walked to the kitchen.

Nate said, "I don't understand that boy. He's wasting his potential."

"I know, Nate. What can we do? Nash has always been stubborn."

I stood in the doorway when Pat noticed me.

"Maggie. How were midterms?" She tried to regain her composure.

"Stressful." I walked into the kitchen. "What was that about?"

"Oh, nothing. We were discussing futures," Pat said

"The conversation is none of my business, but you're pushing Nash in the wrong direction," I said.

"Maggie, you mean well, but let us handle our boy," Nate said.

"I would love to have parents like you while growing up. Sometimes, a child's dream and a parent's dream differ. My parents didn't care about my dreams. They only cared about themselves and money. I would prefer them to yell at me about my dreams. At least I knew that they cared." I walked away.

"What's that supposed to mean?" He asked Pat.

"She loves and cares about our son. She sees something that we're missing."

"Like what?"

"That Nash's dream differs from ours." She shrugged.

*****

I searched for Nash. It would be more challenging until I remembered the find my phone app that Nixon had used to find him. I used that, leading me right to him. He was in a park leaning forwards on a wall.

I walked over and stood next to him.

"How did you find me?"

"Find my phone app." I grinned.

"I need to turn that feature off."

"Do you want to talk about it?"

"Nope."

"Okay. Did you want to hear about midterms?"

He said nothing.

"I'll tell you. Midterms were rough, but I did well."

"Maggie, I prefer not to talk right now."

"That won't happen, Nash."

He sighed. "What do you want from me?"

"I want you to be honest and tell your parents that you want to pursue art."

"They would never approve because it's not a stable job with benefits and a 401k."

"How do you know? Did you ever tell them?"

"Well, no."

"Then you don't know. Nash, I get the entire security reason, but you need to be happy."

"Maggie, you mean well, but stay out of it."

"Fine. Keep being miserable. It's what you do best. Better yet, run away. You're good at running." I walked away.

"Yeah, well, look, who's running now!"

"I'm walking, not running! Enormous difference!"

Well, I tried. I swear these Gray boys were stubborn. None of them could admit to anything. Is it that difficult to fight for something that you love to do?

I'll never understand guys or the Gray brothers.

When I returned, I headed to my room. I wanted to sleep from studying so much. Then I got mixed up in the family drama. When will I ever learn? The way I'm going, never.

CHAPTER 39

SPRING BREAK WITH THE GRAYS

Maggie

The Gray house became tense after that day, and Nash wasn't talking to anyone. He's a big baby.

We received our midterm results and had passed, which meant we were going somewhere for spring break! It's better than getting stuck at home. Nolan had to stay home. Nolan's Valentine's Day escapade still miffed Nate and Pat. I couldn't blame them.

For spring break, we were traveling to Mexico. The trust legalities had tied up my money. Who knows when the courts will release my money? Nate and Pat helped me with my expenses. If that money became mine, I would pay them back—stupid, greedy birth parents.

*****

I was packing when Nash walked into my room. He said nothing but grabbed my hand and led me out of the room. What now?

We left the house and got into the car. Then he drove to a secluded area. Once we parked, we sat in the car. The silence wasn't uncomfortable whatsoever.

"I'm sorry." He stared at his hands resting on the steering wheel.

I hope he makes my death quick.

"You were looking out for me. I took my frustration out on you."

I breathed a sigh of relief. "Thank God because I thought you would kill me, then bury me."

He furrowed his brows at me.

"What? You drove me to no-man's-land. You could have apologized in my room."

Then he started laughing. "I love you."

"Better than hating me." I shrugged.

"I am sorry, though."

"I know, but you need to tell your parents. Nash, you have a gift. Don't waste it."

"I will, but I want to do something else." He pulled me to him and started kissing me. Our kissing got heated as we struggled to get out of our pants. Before anything happened, he made sure he used protection. We're not having babies yet.

Then he was thrusting inside of me. I let out a gasp as he moved. It wasn't like it was nice and slow. I clenched his shirt as he continued to thrust inside me repeatedly as he kissed me. I let out a groan as he did too. We both exploded together.

Our breathing had become heavy.

"I like makeup sex."

He chuckled. "Yeah, but I prefer not to have makeup sex often. I would prefer nice, loving sex." Nash smiled. "I love you, Mags."

"I love you, too, Nash."

He gave me another kiss. Then we got dressed. He took us back to the house. Nash would be okay no matter what happened, but he needed to talk to his parents.

*****

We packed for our trip. Nolan whined about not going. His brothers reminded him to pick a girl whom the police wouldn't raid her house. I thought that was a dumb way of putting it. The Grays could make those comments.

Eight of us traveled to Mexico with the four boys and the four girls. Before we left, we received a lecture from Nate and Pat. Do nothing stupid, don't go to jail, and don't get knocked up. I guess drinking wasn't a big deal to them.

We flew to a Mexican resort. Since I had never flown, this was a treat. I was so nervous that I started laughing when we were landing. The others thought I became possessed, except my head didn't spin around, and I didn't spew green stuff everywhere.

Once we got off the plane, I hugged the ground. Yeah, I wasn't a fan of flying. After Nash peeled me from the asphalt, we checked into our hotel rooms. The best part was that we got to share rooms. Okay, I love spring break.

After getting settled, we grabbed food. Rule of thumb. If you are ever in Mexico, do not, I repeat, do not drink the water. You'll spend more time in the bathroom than out of it. Yes, I learned the hard way when I drank my glass of water at dinner. Within a half-hour, my stomach cramped. Yeah, it wasn't pretty. I thought I would die.

That night I spent time getting acquainted with the porcelain throne. Please, let the rest of the spring break be much better.

*****

The next day, I felt better. Well, after Nash got me medicine for my stomach. I received a ribbing from the brothers. Good times, I tell you.

We hit the beach to have some fun. I burn like a mofo. Even while wearing sunblock, I fry. I always have and always will. Who the heck burns when a person has brown hair? That would be me, that's who.

I spent the entire day in the sun and didn't realize how red I had become.

"Um, Mags, we should go in."

"Nash, I'm having fun."

"Yeah, but your skin doesn't look good." Noah referred to my skin's redness.

"It's fine," I told the brothers.

"Oh, yeah?" Nixon pressed on my skin.

I screamed. "Why did you do that?"

"Well, since you look like a lobster, I was proving a point." He smirked.

I glared at him.

"Come on, Red Lobster. Let's head to the room." Nash guided me back to the hotel without touching me.

Nash bought me Solarcaine. I stripped off my clothes. God, I was so burned. He applied the green goo to my skin and slathered me with it. So much for romance.

I wouldn't be leaving my room for two days.

*****

For the next couple of days, I stayed in my room alone. I won't let Nash stay and not have any fun. Bull, I would. Misery loves company.

I ended up watching Spanish shows on TV. It would be fine if I knew Spanish, but I didn't. I took French. I'll admit Spanish soap operas were funny because they're so dramatic.

While watching a program that I didn't understand, Nash came into the room as I lay there. He stopped and glanced at the TV. "What are you watching?"

"A Spanish soap opera. Javier found out Maria was having an affair with his brother, Jose, and might be pregnant."

"How do you know that?"

"I'm guessing." I grinned.

Nash rolled his eyes. "How's the sunburn?"

"It hurts."

"Okay, let me lather you again." He grabbed the Solarcaine and squeezed a bunch of goo into his palm. He climbed onto the bed and started applying the green goo. It would be hot if I didn't hurt so much.

As he made his way down my body, his hand caressed my inner thigh. Screw the pain. I was getting hot and bothered. My lower half twitched.

"Someone is getting excited."

"Who me? Psh, no."

He continued rubbing the goo on me. Each time he touched my inner thigh, my body reacted. "Hmm, were you sure?"

"Yep, I'm sure."

His hand grazed my nether regions, and a soft moan escaped my lips.

"Well, your body is telling me otherwise." He smirked—curse you, body.

He kneeled, pushed down his shorts, and reached for protection. I whimpered. Being naked and beet red, he couldn't see me blush. He moved my legs apart and positioned himself between them. Then he slid into me as I let out a moan. I tried not to move too much, so my skin wouldn't hurt.

As he thrust inside me, my body was fiery from the sun and hot from Nash. He was careful not to touch me. He pushed inside of me, making me let out a loud moan as I found my release, and he followed suit.

"Damn, that was hot."

"You're telling me."

We laughed at the irony.

*****

After two days, I was no longer in pain but looked ridiculous. I got to endure teasing from the boys because of my redness. If I get married, I'm not going to Mexico or any tropical climate.

The rest of the spring break was beautiful, and Nash and I got reacquainted. He brought much protection, and none of us got arrested. Thank God.

CHAPTER 40

SENIOR SKIP DAY

Maggie

At school, the principal cautioned us about senior skip day. If we didn't show up, we wouldn't graduate. So, what did we do? We skipped. We're seniors, for crying out loud! It's a rite of passage for us.

We headed to Cedar Point for the day. No school, many rides, and junk food makes for an exciting and fun time. Nash, Nixon, Kat, Marcy, Macey, and I went.

We hit the park, running and getting to the best rides. Seniors filled Cedar Point. We didn't travel a billion years to get there.

After riding some rides for a few hours, we took a break to eat. We sat at a table and ate slices of pizza.

Nash said, "I've been thinking about what we had discussed."

"What's that? We had discussed many things."

"My future."

"Okay, I'm all ears." I grinned.

"I don't want to waste my life doing an office job. I want to be happy, so I'm going to school for art."

"That's great! I'm so excited for you. Did you tell your parents?"

"Well…"

"Nash! You need to tell them."

"What if they think the idea is stupid?"

"You say, Ma and Dad, I've decided not to waste my life while working an office job. I'll waste my life with my outstanding girlfriend at school while earning an art degree." I gave him a silly look.

He laughed. "Okay, on one condition."

"What's that?"

"You tell them." He got up and ran.

"Nash! That was a dirty trick!" I got up and ran after him.

After catching up with him, I jumped on his back. He looped his arms around my legs and gave me a piggyback.

We rode the roller coasters, then the spinning rides. We got off the Scrambler, found a garbage can, and tossed our cookies. Ugh, never eat, then go on a spinning ride.

We caught up with the others.

"It's weird not having Nathan and Noah here," Nixon said.

"Yeah, but we can't help it if they're not seniors yet," Nash said.

"Well, I wish your brothers were here," Marcy said.

"What will you do when you girls are in college, and the demon spawns are still in high school?" Nixon asked.

"Psh, commute," Macey said.

"Let me guess. The demon spawns tickle your fancy," Nixon said.

"Who says fancy?" Kat asked him.

"Fancy. Clit. It's the same thing." He shrugged.

"Um, no. You need to retake anatomy because you don't understand a girl's body."

"Well, I understand your body, now, don't I?" He gave her a coy look.

"That is questionable." Kat walked away.

"What do you mean that's questionable?" He chased after her.

"I see those two getting married," I told Nash while leaning into him.

"I do, too

I giggled.

"Come on. Let's go on the Ferris wheel." He held out his hand.

"Oh, no! I hate the Ferris wheel!"

"Since when? You rode the Ferris wheel at the carnival and didn't have any issues."

"Since forever. I didn't tell you."

"Trust me. You'll love this." Nash gave me a wink and a smile.

"Fine." I took his hand.

He dragged me to the Ferris wheel, which I was not too fond of. We got into one bucket. Once everyone was on, they started the ride. I buried my face into Nash as he chuckled. I'm glad he found amusement in my fear.

Then the ride stopped at the top. Oh, God, we'll die! Goodbye, cold, cruel world. It was nice knowing you. Wait a minute. I didn't even go to the prom or graduate yet. Well, this sucks.

"Mags, open your eyes."

I buried my face into his shirt. "No! We'll die."

"We won't die. Stop being so damn dramatic."

"Easy for you to say. But when we plunged to our death, and you were like, we won't die, I'll say I told you so."

"How will you say that if you're dead?"

"Good point. As a ghost, I'll say I told you."

"Will you shut up?" Nixon asked from the bucket below us.

"Why don't you bite me?" I asked.

"I don't bite anything that looks that bad."

"Your brother is something else. As I was saying, when we die, I'll come back and haunt you."

"Then, you'll miss the surprise I have for you."

Surprise? What surprise? I lifted my head, looking around until I saw it. In his fingers, he held a ring. I stared at it. It was white gold with pink diamonds. The sun hit it, making it sparkle like Edward from Twilight. Don't judge. Team Edward all the way.

I stared at it in awe.

"Mags, before you get any ideas, it's not an engagement ring. It's a promise ring."

I turned to him. Shock replaced fear.

"I wanted to give this ring to you, waiting for the right time. Mags, I want to give you the world. I promise to love you forever if you promise to do the same."

I didn't know what to say. Nash promised me so much. I thought about us as we grew up together. I had known Nash my entire life. He was the first boy I had liked before my crush on Bryson. So much had happened between us. I still couldn't believe we were together.

"Say something."

I touched his cheek and gave him a soft kiss while surprising him. "Yes."

A smile curled upon his lips after hearing the word escape my lips. It's a word with so much meaning for us. He took my hand, slid the ring onto my finger, and pulled me into a kiss. As we kissed, the Ferris wheel started.

Sometimes, you must face your fears to find happiness, or it'll destine you to listen to Nixon forever. Nash makes me happy. It's better than listening to Nixon. Trust me. It's never pretty.

CHAPTER 41

PROM

Maggie

We headed into the home stretch of our senior year. My classmates were idiots. They choose the Sunday of Memorial weekend to hold a prom. Who does that?

I wore a black cocktail dress and didn't go the classic route with a big, poofy dress. I wanted to keep it simple, although the heels I bought were too big. Ugh, I love these shoes. Pat fixed them for me so that I could wear them. She shoved toilet paper in the toes of my dress shoes.

Kat fixed my hair and makeup while the guys got dressed in their tuxes. I couldn't wait. This dance would be much better than the last school dances. At least, I hope so.

"Girls! Hurry, or you'll miss your prom!" Nate said.

We finished and headed downstairs to see the boys dressed in their tuxes while waiting for us. I walked over to Nash.

"Why is your slip showing?"

"It's not a slip. It's part of the dress and made that way."

"If you say so."

I smacked him as he chuckled.

Someone knocked on the door.

"I got it." Nolan said, answering the front door to find a girl standing there. It's not any girl but a senior girl, making us do a double-take.

"Well, hello, handsome." She gave Nolan a seductive look.

"Hey, Lucy."

"Ready?"

"Absolutely." He held out his arm as she took it.

"Did our baby brother score a date with the hottest senior at school?" Nathan asked.

"Yep," Noah said.

The demon spawn earned a smack from Marcy and Macey.

"The young'un likes older women. That's a change," Nixon said.

We gave Nixon a look as he shrugged.

We were off to our senior prom.

*****

We arrived, exited the limo, and headed inside. The music blared while people danced. Nash took my hand and led me to the dance floor.

He pulled me to him, and we danced. It was like we were dancing in the air. He held me as we danced.

"Imagine us dancing when we get married."

I gave him a weird expression.

"Don't worry. I'll ask you when the time is right. We have plenty of time."

I laughed, as he did too. We continued to dance until we took a break to get something to drink. The others joined us as Bryson walked up to me. This encounter would not end well.

"Maggie?"

I turned to face him. Nash wrapped his arm around my waist.

"I wanted to apologize to you."

"You broke my nose."

"I know, and I'm sorry."

"You're sorry? You humiliated me at homecoming. You broke my nose in the hallway. You made me think that I was this horrible person for liking you, and you're sorry."

"Mags," Nash said.

I turned to Nash. "No." I turned back to Bryson and stepped toward him. "I wasted four years of my life on you. I had a stupid crush. I thought Bryson Tilson was the end all, be all. You humiliated me and broke my nose. For what? Because I liked you. That's the problem with guys. You take an innocent girl who shows an interest in you, making her life difficult. Why? So, you can feel better about yourself. The sad part is you will never notice a great girl. Someone else will see a great girl. Then it's too late for you. Save your apology, Bryson, because whatever feelings I had for you are over. I have someone who loves me, and I love him. That's way more important than a stupid high school crush." I turned and walked back to Nash. "To answer your question from earlier. Yes, I can imagine dancing at our wedding."

He wrapped an arm around my waist, pulled me to him, and then gave me a mind-blowing kiss. He took my hand and led me back to the dance floor. The others followed, leaving Bryson stunned.

Crushes don't last. One day, you'll wake up and understand why it never worked out with anyone else. A wise person told me that when I had a broken heart. That person picked up the pieces.

We danced most of the night. It's a night I'll never forget. I don't think any of us would forget that night.

After prom, we hung out at the Gray's house. I kicked off my shoes. Putting toilet tissue in my dress shoes wasn't a superb idea. My toes hurt. I rubbed my feet as Nash took my feet and massaged them.

"I must hand it to you, Maggie. You grew some balls since we started the year," Nixon said.

"I swear you need to take another anatomy course." Kat sighed and shook her head.

"Yeah, that was outstanding," Nathan said.

"I feel good. I'm not afraid anymore." I smiled. "I have a question. Why did you guys hate me so much when I got here?"

The brothers glanced at each other. It was the elephant in the room that needed addressing.

"We didn't hate you," Noah said.

"Are you sure? What you said and did prove otherwise."

"How so?" Nathan asked me.

"Nolan stole my bra. You both read my journal, then read it to the entire school. Nixon called me a creeper while Nash kicked me out of his bedroom. So, yeah, I would say you guys hated me."

They started laughing.

Nixon said, "Wow, you missed the point."

"Huh? And what's so funny?"

Nash tapped my foot. "I kicked you out of my bedroom because I liked you and didn't know how to tell you. And well, you're hot."

"I only called you names because that's what brothers do when they tease their sister," Nixon said.

"We read your journal because that's what brothers do to their sister. You told the school we were gay and had the Clap," Nathan said.

Noah nodded in agreement.

"Well, you had to admit that was funny." I giggled.

"And I stole your underwear because that's what brothers do to annoy their sisters," Nolan said.

I gave Nolan a skeptical look. "What brother does that? Because I'm sure no brother does."

"Okay, brothers, don't do that. I enjoy a good panty raid." He smirked.

"Nolan! You're a freaking perv!" Nixon smacked Nolan on the back of his head.

"Mags, you're like a sister to my brothers. They consider you a sister. It'll work out when I make you their sister," Nash said.

The brothers nodded.

"Maggie, we don't hate you. We love you. You're the sister that we never had," Nixon said.

"I guess I never looked at it that way," I said.

The things that we did to each other made sense. We're siblings who fought with each other but loved each other. I dragged the brothers into situations, proving I was a sister to them.

I didn't ask for brothers but ended up with them. Yes, they're a pain in the ass. But I love them.

CHAPTER 42

FINALS AND OTHER LIFE DECISIONS

Maggie

Finals were happening for us. Nixon and I had short days because we're seniors. We had commencement practices, along with the girls.

After my final, I walked out of the classroom and saw Nixon. I ran over to him. He picked me up and swung me around.

"We did it!" He earned shushes from the teachers.

"We did it."

"Come on. Let's find the girls."

We ran until we found the girls' classrooms and waved. Kat was finishing up. She got up and handed in her final, then exited the room. She jumped on Nixon, and he kissed her. Next was Marcy. The three of us waved as she nodded. She finished, turned in her final, and left. We made our way to Macey's classroom. We plastered ourselves against the glass in the door as she laughed and rolled her eyes.

Macey finished and joined us. "You guys are nuts."

"Who cares? We finished high school," Nixon said.

We walked to the entrance, and I took one last look. High school was over. It's time to graduate and start a new chapter of my life with the Gray brothers and Nash.

I walked out of the school to find Nash leaning against his car, waiting for me. I started walking towards him and broke out into a run. I jumped into his arms after reaching him as he spun me around.

"You did it, baby girl. I'm so proud of you." Nash beamed.

I smiled, then kissed him.

"Come on. We're meeting everyone for lunch. But first, I need to make a stop." Nash set me down.

*****

We pulled up to a factory and got out of the car. Nash walked up to the door. I followed him as we passed machines, along with offices. He walked to a door and knocked.

Nate turned around. "Nash? What's up?"

"Is Ma around?"

"Yeah, she's checking on a shipment. She'll be right back."

"Those idiots! Can't they get anything right?" A voice said.

"Never mind. Your mom is on her way back."

Pat entered and walked over to Nate. "Nathaniel, you need to have a word with the shipping manager. He received the wrong shipment, so it must go back."

"I'll make a call in a few minutes, but we have company." He nodded at us.

Pat turned and smiled. "Oh, hey, kids. What brings you to our neck of the woods?"

"Remember when you wanted me to find direction in my life?" Nash asked.

"Yes," they said.

"Well, I made a decision."

"And?" Nate asked.

"Well." He turned and pushed me forward. "Mags will tell you." He hid behind me.

I turned to him. "Coward."

He shrugged.

I shook my head, rolled my eyes, and then turned back to them. "Nash wants to pursue an art degree."

They both stood there. I didn't know if what I said was okay. You can never tell with Nate and Pat.

"Okay, they're not saying anything," Nash said.

"I stunned them into silence," I said.

"This might be bad. We'll make a run for it."

"I agree."

We crept out of the office.

Then someone said, "Art, huh?"

We stopped, straightened up, and turned around.

"Well, at least it's something," Nate said.

"Wait. You're not mad?" Nash asked him.

"No. Should I be?"

"Well, most parents consider art a waste of time."

"Hun, we're not most parents. Did you hit your head or something?" Pat asked Nash.

"No."

"Are you sure? Because you forget our last name is Gray."

"I'm confused."

"I am, too," I said.

"Nash Nathaniel Gray! You should know better than anyone that we'll support you and your brothers if you follow your dreams. It's better than being a hobo!" Pat said.

"Yeah, hobos are dirty and smelly. Girls don't dig them," Nate said.

"Nathaniel Mark!"

"What? I'm just saying. Don't be a hobo, Nash." Nate nodded his head and winked.

"Ignore your father. His mother dropped him on his head as a kid."

"She did not! Stop telling lies, woman!"

"Yes, she did," she mouthed while pointing at Nate and making faces.

"You're going to school for art. Great! Now, can we get back to work? I need to hurt a shipping manager!" Nate said.

We left as Nate and Pat argued about work. These people might be my in-laws one day. Oh, boy.

We left the factory and met the others. I guess life was moving in the right direction for everyone. Why would it get interesting?

CHAPTER 43

GRADUATION

Maggie

We practiced commencement for three days. The principal thought we would screw up graduation. We're not apes and can follow instructions. Well, most of us can.

We collected our caps and gowns. I hung mine on the back of my closet door.

Nash tapped on my door.

"Hey."

He walked over to me. "Are you ready for tomorrow?"

"Yeah. Is Nixon ready?"

Nixon said, "Woohoo! I'm graduating!"

"I would say yes," Nash said.

I laughed.

"Come on."

"Where are we going?"

"You'll see." Nash took my hand and led me out of my room.

*****

Nash pulled into an open field and parked the car. We got out of the vehicle as he popped the trunk and pulled out a picnic basket and a blanket.

"Look at you, Mr. Romantic." I smiled.

"I thought we'd enjoy a picnic." He walked over to a spot and set the basket down. Then he opened the blanket and laid it down. He joined me and pulled out sandwiches, chips, and beverages.

We sat on the blanket and talked. Afterward, we lay on our backs while looking at the clouds.

"This was perfect. Thank you."

"Sometimes, you need simplicity."

"What will happen to us?"

"Well, I figure we'll graduate, get married, and have babies. Maybe a little Nash or a little Mags running around."

I saw a little boy with chestnut brown hair and steel-grey eyes running around. Nash picked him up and swung him around. It was at that moment that Nash would become my family.

I placed my hand on his cheek, then leaned over and kissed him. He pulled me to him while rolling me onto my back. He kissed me, then said, "But no babies until we're married."

"No worries there." I smiled.

He kissed me again.

*****

The next day, we rushed to get ready.

"Nixon and Maggie, hurry! Graduation starts in thirty minutes!" Nate said.

"We're getting dressed, old man! Calm your tits!" Nixon said.

"I'll give you, old man! And I do not have tits!"

Nash knocked on my door. "You better hurry before my dad has a stroke."

I stood up straight after pinning my cap to my hair. I turned around. "Well, does grey suit me?"

He studied me while picturing me when I was little, following him around, and he would run over my Barbie dolls. Later, when I became a teen, entering my gawky period. My braces had come off at fifteen. My face had cleared up. He returned to find me asleep in his bed.

He remembered our late-night talks through my window. Our shopping trips. The ice cream fights, first dance, first kiss, first date, and the first time. He gazed at me as I stood in my cap and gown.

"Nash?"

"Um, yeah." He wiped his eyes.

I walked over to him and smiled. "Are you crying?"

"No. I had something in my eyes."

I raised my brows. "Yeah, your eyeballs."

He laughed. "I remembered moments."

"And?"

"And I love you. Now let's get you graduated." Nash pulled me into a kiss.

Nate said, "Two seconds!"

Nash chuckled and took my hand. "Way to ruin a moment, Dad!"

*****

We arrived on time and found our seats. We sat in our seats and listened to the faculty speak, which was annoying. The salutatorian spoke and wasn't too bad. Then the valedictorian got up and spoke. If you ever attended a graduation, the valedictorian is number one in the class. The person gives a long-ass speech.

They give a speech about our high school experience and the future. High school sucks with teachers you don't like. Your classmates are decent, while some are jerky. Don't be jerky.

Our valedictorian was that kid who gave the most boring speech I have ever heard. Nixon and I groaned. Their speech rambled on forever. Someone, please put us out of our misery. The principal cut off the valedictorian. Thank God.

The principal called us to collect our diplomas. When Nixon got called, the Grays whistled and cheered. They did the same thing when they called my name, especially Nash. Ah, can't you feel the love?

After they called each senior, we moved our tassels and proclaimed that we had graduated. Then we tossed our caps into the air even though the school said no. We didn't listen. Yep, we were in that class.

After graduation, we met up and hugged. It was a beautiful day. The day could not have been better. I couldn't wait for the future, which would bring more chaos and antics. What do you expect from the Gray brothers?

CHAPTER 44

GUESS WHO?

Maggie

After graduation, we let loose during the summer.

"Nolan! Give me back my bra, you brat!" I chased Nolan down the hall, only for Nash to walk by and snatch my bra from Nolan's hands.

"Aw, Nash, you're no fun!"

"Leave my girlfriend's underwear alone, you perv!"

Nolan grumbled as Nash handed my bra back to me. I kissed him and plodded to my room to find Nathan and Noah reading my journal.

"Oh, Nash is so dreamy. The way he kisses me. I can't wait to have his hands," Nathan said.

I snatched my journal out of Nathan's hands.

"Aw, come on! We were getting to the excellent parts!"

"What have I told you about reading my journal?" I smacked Nathan.

"I thought you were burning your journal?" Noah asked me.

I glared at him. "Get out!" I pointed at the door.

"You're no fun," Nathan said.

The demon spawn left the room.

Thick sole shoes clunked up the stairs. Oh, great. Nixon was home. I popped my head out of my door.

"What?" He gave me an annoyed face.

"Nothing." I shrugged.

"Stop looking at me like that! It's creepy!"

"You're creepy! Stop being a whiny crybaby." I stuck my tongue out at him.

He returned the favor.

Someone yanked me out of my room, picked me up, and tossed me onto a bed. Well, okay, then.

"Why must you annoy my brothers?" Nash asked me.

"Because that's what sisters do." I smirked.

He pulled me into a kiss, then stared at me.

"Take a picture. It'll last longer."

He rolled his eyes. I giggled before his lips came crashing onto mine.

Life was back to normal. The boys drove me crazy, and I drove them crazy, but we're crazy together. Oh, did I forget to mention that Nate and Pat were taking the family on vacation as a graduation gift for the summer? They wanted to spend time with everyone before life became hectic. I couldn't wait.

The doorbell rang. We stuck our heads out of our doorways and investigated the hallway. Then the doorbell rang again. Who was at the front door?

We made our way downstairs and watched. Pat came out of the kitchen.

Nate opened the door. "Jonas? Cayson? What are you doing here?"

"Weren't you the one that invited us to go on vacation with you?" Jonas asked him.

"Well, yeah."

"Well, here we are. And we brought our families, too." Cayson grinned.

The brothers and I glanced at each other. Nate looked at us, then back at his brothers. There goes the neighborhood. God, save us.

To continue in The Gray Brothers: It's All Relative.